KEEPERS OF THE STAR PATH

LEGENDS OF STAR JUNCTION
BOOK 2

SERRA WILDHEART

Scribe Hive
Publishing

Keepers of the Star Path

Series: Legends of Star Junction

Serra Wildheart

Copyright © 2025

ISBN Paperback: 978-1-962112-21-5

ISBN Ebook: 978-1-962112-22-2

Cover design by: Medeiros Creative

Published through Scribe Hive Publishing LLC

Pueblo, CO

www.scribehivepublishing.com

A women-owned publishing cooperative driven to share great stories that want to be told.

CONTENTS

PROLOGUE

Not so long ago, on a night without clouds, the elders and the children sat around the talking fire. The fire and the stars provided enough light to see all the faces clearly, down to the wrinkles of the sages and the light in their eyes. They sat with the children, teaching them with stories about the stars and the time that would come—a time much like now. On this night, elders, teachers, beloved leaders, and healers shared the wisdom for the time to come so that each child would know their role, their importance, and the love and light they always held within and shared.

One of these fires took place at the Star Junction in the southwest of what had become known as the United States. Nestled somewhere near high desert, alpine forests, and a great canyon, this special place was protected by the mountains and secluded by ponderosa pine and aspen forests. Even now, the road there takes time and focus to drive. Back then it was a simple, two-way path traveled with patience and intention. But highways had made connection and the community was beginning to change with outside influence and the new industry of more accessible, neighboring towns, not just at this Star Junction, but at those all over the earth. It was time to put the play in motion, plant the remaining seeds, and teach each child well how to navigate in the world.

The elders spoke with magic in their voices. This was not a time for fear but for understanding, for imbuing the young ones with possibility, imagination, and the light of the stars. Some even sang the messages, for this was not a prophecy of warning but of action.

Beautiful children, you are the seeds. Life will take you many directions. When it does, you must always remember the truth of who you are, the essence of your being, the love within. You must never forget how to call the stars home. How to listen without ears. How to teach the next generations to teach the ones who come to help the world to remember. You have been here before, and you must remember all of it, as best you can. You will face many distractions and choices. Remember, each choice changes the next options. Know thyself. Know thy truth. Know thy source. And your choices will always be clear.

Some of the young ones remained in the towns and junctions where they were born and learned the ways of generations. Many were called to travel to bigger cities by trains and even across the oceans to new lands altogether. The hope for the lessons that each, even during their darkest times, would know to call to the stars to light the path.

Events of the world—war, economic depression, droughts, modern convenience, and the promise of opportunity—had caused many to leave and move to new places. The idea that something better lay just on the other side of the fence, or country, or world, had become a compelling force chiseling away at communities and towns. But for the children sitting around the fires that night, the illusion was clear. So was their journey. They would walk the path that covered great distances—the path of the stars—understanding it would eventually lead them all home.

Maren was one of the older children around the fire that night in Star Junction. She was nearly seventeen and was looked up to by many of the younger children, the girls especially but not exclusively. Maren was confident, compassionate, and always kind to the younger kids. She had become very close with one of the youngest of the group at the fire that night.

Eliaflore was not quite five and was one of the most attentive of the group. She and Maren were close enough that young Flor felt Maren's distraction and the sadness in her heart. Eliaflore came up to Maren, holding each of her hands and linking gazes. Maren's eyes glistened with tears as she smiled softly.

"My dear Eliaflore, the beautiful, wise flower, you always know. We are leaving tomorrow. My heart is broken." Eliaflore squeezed her hands tighter as her own tears formed, and she began to dance with Maren. They danced with the fire and through the tears, proving that sorrow and love could share the same space and somehow transform into bits of joy. Maren vowed that if she could not return to Star Junction herself one day, her children would. They would know this place in their hearts and consider it home—even if they were on the other side of the earth. It was her promise to the fire, the stars, and her family.

Other children danced too. Some sang with the drums, songs of resonance and ethereal tones. A few sat quietly, not called to move or do anything more. They sat, listened, enjoyed. The elders watched over them all until it was time for all to return home for the night and rest.

In the morning Maren's family gathered around the car that had come to drive them to the train station three or four hours away. The car wasn't the first one to come to Star Junction, but it was a rare occurrence, happening seldom enough that the noise of the engine and the dust kicked up on the dirt road signaled to the people that it was time.

Most of the town rose to see their beloved friends off. Sadness lingered in the air. It seemed that hearts broke every time someone, or a family, left Star Junction. Though it was understood that people would leave, and some would come, it was never easy. The town mourned the loss just as it celebrated the life of every being there.

It wasn't that the ones who left didn't love Star Junction. Maren's father and mother had made the decision after much debate and some distress. Her father's family had moved away some time ago and sent many invitations as well as alluring descriptions of the opportunities to be had and the expanded life for the kids. Her father had begun traveling to larger cities to work, like Exton, Flagstaff, and even Phoenix. Then his employer offered to move the family to New York. There, they would be near his family. The kids, Maren and her younger sister and brothers, would have so much life open to them. It was exciting. The move was paid for and the decision made.

Eliaflore worked her way through the crowd to see Maren, who had been avoiding eye contact while attempting to hold it all together. When did she become stoic? When did she begin to care if others saw her cry? Eliaflore stood before her and held out a gift wrapped in cloth and tied with the long grass that grew by the river. Maren kneeled to accept the gift, tears freely flowing down her cheeks.

As Maren untied the grass, Eliaflore spoke. "Grandfather helped me make this for you, to help you remember always and carry us with you."

Maren smiled sweetly at Eliaflore and looked back at the bundle as she opened the cloth.

"Ohhh." Taking an audible breath, she paused in awe of what she saw before her. She gently lifted the beautiful pendant with seven tiny crystals of different colors in the pattern of their stars. Their junction of stars. The glass that held them was of the clear night, with the warmth of fire below. "Eliaflore, it is *beautiful*. How did you make it?"

Eliaflore just smiled. "I just asked Spirit what was best for you, and the crystals told me. But Grandfather helped with the glass." Eliaflore took the thin cord attached to it and placed the necklace around Maren's neck. She kissed her on the cheek and wrapped her arms around her. "I will dream with you at night."

Maren wrapped her arms around her young friend. "And I will dream with you." As Maren stood up, she stopped abruptly, taking the bracelet from her wrist. She knelt back down and placed the bracelet on Eliaflore's wrist, wrapping it around twice so it wouldn't fall off. "Now we both have our amulets," she said with a smile.

One of the children from the night before, a boy about seven named Ikenial watched differently than the others. He did not like that people left. In fact, it felt as if they were leaving him personally behind. He watched the car and dreamed of where it could take him. He secretly hoped his family would leave too because these magical items from the world that he heard of—the cars, trains, and even something that flew in the air—all invaded his dreams, and he knew his life must include them. Eliaflore saw him watching their friends drive away and believed his sorrow was the same as hers.

CHAPTER

ONE

S ofia searched for the place of her mother's stories—the one written about in her journals and memory book—that Sofia had never seen but which lived in her imagination as her mother described what had been her own magical childhood home. The place of the seven stars. Sofia vowed at a young age that when she was old enough and able, she would find the place that illuminated her dreams. This was how she came to Star Junction with her husband and son.

Sully was used to city life. Tall buildings, traffic noise, steam from the storm drains, and smells from restaurants and exhaust all created the hum of life for him. But he loved Sofia in his way and was enchanted by her stories of a place she had never been. After she became ill and he lost his job, he agreed to leave the only home he had known to start over. They squeezed what they could into the decade-old 1955, four-door Chevy Nomad and drove. The change in climate and pace was intended to help Sofia recover. He told himself they could always go back.

But things didn't go the way they planned. Sully had worked in city jobs: driving, subways, and even in office maintenance. He was older than Sofia by more than ten years, but still, they were young enough to begin again. When they found Star Junction, it was a shock to Sully's system. He struggled to find a job he could do in a small-town economy and struggled to keep his big city personality a bit quieter so as not to draw attention.

He might as well have been on a different planet. Everything about him felt as if he just didn't fit. Six-foot-three, strong shoulders, and booming voice, Sully felt small in a quiet town filled with people who didn't know him. He immediately missed the "Hey, Sully!" being called from stoops, store fronts, and balconies. The tallest building here was three stories and didn't even have an elevator.

Sofia teased him a little and told him not to worry. It would just take time to get to know people and find the right job. She knew when William started school the next week, they would get to know the other parents and the town. And she couldn't wait to join in on one of the music festival nights she had heard about. "Oh, Sully, we're going to love it."

Their location didn't help them to feel a part of it all. Instead of buying in town, they chose a less expensive, small house that was located a bit up the mountain and sat alone for the most part. Most people had long ago left the old remote dwellings in favor of the community of the town that had developed below. They mostly used the old farm properties as work spaces for any farming they needed to do. The small dwellings became temporary shelters and housing for equipment and sorting spots for harvest. Many of them had collapsed or been reclaimed by nature, but with limited resources, one of these was all Sofia and Sully could afford at the time.

The distance seemed to grow with time. The drive to town didn't take more than a few minutes, but the realization that they had no neighbors dawned and kept them feeling outside of life there. And kept others from receiving them. However, William thrived at first. The boy quickly discovered trails and paths to explore as well as a walking route into town that only took thirty minutes. He had never seen so many trees that he could actually touch and smell and climb.

"Dad, come with me! It's incredible!" But Sully was not inclined toward nature.

―――

Sofia and William arrived at the school early. She wondered if this building was old enough to have been the one her mother had learned in. It looked as if it had been added onto and there was a second building that seemed much newer. But this one could hold her mother's memories. Sofia closed her eyes and tried to feel for her.

William looked around with anticipation as he thought of all his grandmother's stories. This school was quite a bit smaller than the one he had attended in the city. They walked down the hall to the office, passing classrooms and glass displays of art, rocks, and historical tools. They stopped in their tracks as they turned the corner. The wall facing them was a mosaic of tile pieces, glass, beads, and what looked like grains and grasses. Some of the beads and glass sparkled as stars in the night sky. All of the elements were pieced together to depict the mountain, a giant eye, the pavilion from the park, and a fire almost tall enough to reach the sky. William and Sofia were both mesmerized. They stood, motionless, until a well-dressed man approached and greeted them, interrupting their daydreaming.

"Hello. Welcome. I'm Mr. Samuels, the principal here at Star Junction Elementary."

Sofia turned to face him briefly "Oh, thank you." She couldn't help but to look back at the mosaic.

He smiled, understanding the beauty of the wall. "It is striking. Isn't it? Powerful, really."

"Yes..." Sofia suddenly snapped out of it and composed herself. "Oh dear, I am so sorry. I don't know what came over me." She smiled a disarming and sweet smile. "I am Sofia. I called before to enroll my son. This is William."

"Ah yes, welcome. William, it is a pleasure to meet you. I'm sure you will enjoy it here."

William shook Mr. Samuels' hand as his father had taught him, firm and strong.

"Thank you, sir." Mr. Samuels smiled and nodded his approval. "Sir, who made the wall?"

"That is a good question. This mosaic was created by our town artisans when this building was first constructed over a hundred years ago. I can tell you that our little town is filled with artisans. You will learn more about it as a student here and part of our community."

"Mom, did Grandma mention this in her stories?"

Mr. Samuels was quick to respond. "Is your grandmother from here?"

Sofia answered, "Yes, my mother, Maren, was born here. She left when she was young but always wanted to return."

"Ahh, Maren. Wonderful. She was much-loved here. I was just a boy—younger than William—when her family moved away. But I remember us all gathering around to see her and her family off." He smiled as he paused. "This means you are children of Star Junction. Welcome home."

Sofia smiled. She had dreamed of this place for so long. Finally arriving felt like a piece of life falling into place.

Crowds were just beginning to arrive for the Friday fire at the Star Pavilion. Every week the townspeople gathered, shared food, played music, and danced around a fire. Flor was setting up the fire pit and giving instructions to the helpers and the musicians. As she was surveying the crowds, she noticed a boy watching the food tables. He perched himself next to the oak tree they called Sir—an ancient oak older than most of the town.

Flor thought his choice was a wise one. Sir was a tree full of wisdom and big enough for a boy to feel hidden from view if he stood beneath it and perhaps tucked to the side. The boy wore a short-sleeved plaid shirt and jeans. He appeared to be Edward's age, perhaps ten or eleven, but haggard. Even from the distance, Flor saw this boy fully and knew he was a child of Star Junction. Without knowing why, she felt him a part of her family.

She watched him stalk his prey, staying invisible and waiting for the right moment. He hung back until people at the tables were distracted or enough others lingered around to blend in with. He was hungry. He planned to eat quickly and grab as much food as he could carry to take home. The boy thought he had to sneak it. He didn't know that all were welcome to come and to take what they needed.

Flor suspected who he was, part of a new family to town, but she hadn't met him or his family yet. As she finished providing directions and the festivities were beginning, she found Mr. Samuels and inquired about the boy.

"Ah, yes. His name is William. He arrived at the school this year. Fifth grade. Same class as Edward. He started off quite well but lately seems to be struggling, I'm afraid."

"I see. Do you know why that could be?" Flor asked.

"Yes, I thought you would know. Unfortunately, his mother has fallen ill. I'm not sure his father is coping well, but the boy seems to have clean clothes and still shows up to school. He just, well, doesn't socialize with the other children and barely does his work." Mr. Samuels was a kind man with good intentions and a tendency to forget to share important discoveries. He and Flor had known each other since childhood. Most families in Star Junction had been there for generations.

"Thank you, Mr. Samuels. This is very helpful. I wish I had known sooner." Flor had a moment of regret. She hadn't been paying enough attention, and she had let a new family slide past without welcoming them. It had been a particularly busy and distracting couple of months.

"Oh dear, Flor. Forgive me. I should have told you as soon as I met them, but I got caught up in the start of school. His mother, Sofia, is Maren's daughter."

That explained why she felt him as family. Flor turned back to the food tables, but William was gone. She thought how good he was at invisibility and turned her attention back to the festivities. Now that she had seen him and learned who he was, she would listen to understand what was to be done.

———

Sully was suspicious of William's bounty of food and shamed him for stealing. He wasn't sure what made him angrier, stealing or charity. Sully didn't know which it was, but he knew he hadn't provided it. He just needed a break and for Sofia to get better. He knew how to provide for his family, but he didn't know how to heal his wife, how to make her better so she could leave the house and experience the place she had always dreamed of. He didn't know how to find work and watch over her for the last few weeks. She hadn't been out of bed since taking William to school.

The next day Sofia convinced Sully that she could go into town. "Honey, I don't think it's a good idea. Even I can see you aren't well."

"Now, Sully, I want to go to town. I can't stay cooped up in this house. I'll never get better that way." She paused, picked up her purse, and looked at him again in a way he didn't know how to process. "I am not asking."

She wanted desperately to meet people and ask if anyone might have known her mother. To experience this town and place and people in the way Maren had always described. She wasn't going to miss it. If she only had a little time left, she would use it to know Star Junction.

Sully walked over to her, kissed her on the forehead, and brought her into his chest in a loving embrace. It was all he knew to do. "Okay." He grabbed the keys, and they headed for the car. Sully held his arm out for Sofia and walked along with her to the passenger door. He gracefully opened it for her with a wink and a tip of his hat. This had been their routine since their first date. Every door, no matter where they were, he made sure to open for her. William followed quietly and got in the back seat.

It was a beautifully warm fall day. While many of the trees were evergreen, the aspens and oaks did more than their share of expression with the once-green leaves turning golden yellow, a few even turning red. The family drove through the town, turning down every street to take it all in.

Sofia searched her purse for the paper where she had written the address. She wondered how she hadn't remembered to look sooner.

Sully noticed her distress and chimed in, "Honey, you know the streets have probably changed. Your mom said when she was here there weren't even regular roads and no one owned a car."

Sofia's hands stopped and rested on her purse. She stared out the window at the mountain beyond the street and houses.

"Honey?" Sully touched her shoulder, but she kept her eyes on the mountain. He turned and looked at William, gesturing that he should talk.

William leaned forward and put his hands on his mother's shoulders. "Mom..." And then he saw it. The eye from the mosaic. "Whoa..." he said quietly.

Sully thought his whole family had lost their minds.

"What is wrong with you two?"

William pointed toward the eye. Sully looked briefly but couldn't imagine what could be so compelling. Sofia breathed in slowly—the trees, the mountain, her family.

"Oh, Sully, it is all so beautiful. I am okay, dear. This is why we came." She took his hand in hers and squeezed it tightly as a tear gently eased down her cheek.

Sully relaxed some with her hand held tightly. He glanced again at the mountain, sure she was just being sentimental. Just for a second, he thought he saw movement, like an eye closing. He shook off the notion and summoned his courage. "I'm glad you like it. Should we keep going?"

They pulled up alongside the center square to see the Star Pavilion, and Sully kept the engine running. Sofia understood he was trying to protect her limited energy, but she knew in her being, there was nothing to protect. She must see what she came to see now. "Let's get out. I want to be in the Pavilion."

William was relieved. He thought if she could be with his tree and then the pavilion space, she might feel better. He didn't know why he felt this. He waited for his dad's nod and then got out to open Sofia's door.

Sully turned off the engine and came around to walk with Sofia, his right arm around her waist and her left hand in his. William walked by her side. She placed her right hand on his shoulder. *He should be playing*, she thought. If they hadn't come, he would have friends to play with.

They sat quietly, but Sully fidgeted. He was a doer, a man who got things done, took care of everyone, and didn't waste time. He didn't know how to be without his constant ideas and plans, but he couldn't figure out a plan. Maybe they had waited too long to come here. Maybe they shouldn't have come at all. But goddammit, this shouldn't be happening.

Sofia leaned over to him and whispered, "Sully, please be strong. You are the strongest man I've ever known. Our son needs your strength. I love you, and am so grateful to have had you with me."

Sully gulped his sobs back and shook his head.

"Honey, I think I should take you to the hospital now. The one we found. I love you too much to lose you now." He scooped her up in his powerful arms and carried her to the car.

The tiny hospital had just twenty rooms split by a reception desk, waiting room, and small cafeteria. The cafeteria opened to a cozy courtyard with flowers, trees, and benches. The room next to the cafeteria served as a chapel and opened to the courtyard, providing a view of the mountain.

Sofia also had a view of the mountain from her bed, and she made them put the IV where it wouldn't obstruct her view. She found the mountain soothing somehow. It was nothing she could put into words or make anyone else understand. It just—breathed with her. As if it were right there, fully present, holding her hand.

She sent Sully away, doing her best to convince him that all was well. The doctors would take good care of her. She would be okay for a while. He should go take a walk, get some rest, or find a way to release the pressure that was building up inside him. William opted to stay, agreeing to the rules his parents set to stay quiet and respectful in the hospital. No wandering places he didn't belong, so his mother could rest.

Sofia dozed off, and William decided to wander a bit. He wasn't breaking the rule if he didn't go to the wrong places. He quietly walked the hallway, first going into the cafeteria. The quarter in his pocket—the one he received for his birthday so many months before—would cover a soda and snack. He didn't think his parents would mind in this case and maybe wouldn't notice.

Just in case, he went out to the courtyard and examined all the flowers and plants with his soda. There were so many he had never seen before. He found a perch next to an angel trumpet tree. He didn't know why, but he started talking. "Hi, tree. I'm William." The tree stood quietly, her leaves blowing softly in the breeze. "I think my mom would really like you when she gets better..."

His words stopped as his tears flowed out. He must not be strong like his father, because he didn't know how to make them stop. He looked up at the tree and the mountain beyond. "Please, she has to get better." He buried his head into the crux of his elbow and tried to find his breath again.

He noticed warmth on his back, the sun holding him gently. He looked up again to see what was happening. As he wiped his face with his sleeve, he saw a hummingbird dip its long beak into the lengthy flower. She flitted before him, from flower to leaf, her irides-cent feathers glistening in the sunlight. She perched lightly on a thin twig close enough that he could have touched it.

He couldn't take his eyes off of her. She launched again and buzzed his head, circling and flitting back and forth, up and down, before hovering in front of him for moments unmeasured. He smiled for the first time in days. She bounced up and down again and then flew away.

Sofia dozed in and out, awaiting the doctor or nurse or Sully's return. As she awoke to look out at the mountain, Flor stood in the way. Although she was surprised to see someone there, she wasn't star-tled. Flor smiled warmly for her.

"You must be Sofia. I am Flor. Your mother knew me as Eliaflore."

Sofia repeated the words in her head and gave them time to sink in. "You, you knew my mother?"

"You are Maren's daughter, yes?"

"That's right." Sofia smiled. She had been desperate to know any of what her mother had described and to meet anyone who might have known her. "She left so long ago. I didn't know if anyone would remember her."

Flor took Sofia's hands in hers. "Maren is not one to be forgotten. Life took her far from here, but she always remained in the heart of Star Junction."

For the first time since she got sick, since long before they made the drive across the country to find Star Junction, Sofia cried. She cried tears to release the fear and the feelings of shame and weak-ness, to release the guilt she felt for even the possibility that she would not be alive to raise William or to love and take care of Sully. She cried tears for Maren who should have been with them and tears for all the confusion and time spent longing instead of acting. The tears flowed until they were tears of relief for this moment, for this woman's kindness holding her hands, and gratitude for the relief from holding in the tears for so long.

Flor held her in compassion and love, and when she noticed the shift in the tears she continued, "Maren and I danced the fire together. She was quite a bit older than me, but we were sisters in all ways but blood. The day she left I gave her a pendant for her to always have this home, Star Junction, with her. And she gave me this bracelet." As she spoke, she removed the bracelet to show Sofia.

Sofia reached up to the necklace hidden under her gown.

"I tell you all of this for you to know you have family here. I regret that you came and didn't immediately know us, that we didn't provide a proper welcome. Please forgive me for that."

Sofia didn't know what to say or how to respond. She felt as if Flor was reading her mind and doubts about coming. "Of course, you didn't know. I didn't know how to find... anyone."

"You have now. For you, your husband, and your beautiful boy."

"My mom always insisted that he was meant to be here. She made me promise that I would find a way. I've already seen his curiosity grow. But Sully... I'm not sure how he'll do. I've never seen him like this. It is a completely different world from what he knows."

Flor smiled. "Ahh, the world does take on many shapes and sizes. Doesn't it?" She squeezed Sofia's hands. "Your husband will walk his path and make his choices. We will do what we can to help him see the good ones." Flor moved her hand to Sofia's head, gently stroking the hair from her forehead and relaxing her brow. "Maren was always the wisest of us. She saw and listened well that William belonged here. He is a bright light with a heart full of love and a beautiful role to play."

Sofia didn't understand all of what Flor said but suddenly realized that she sounded so much like Maren. Her heart filled up with warmth at the thought. She thought she felt the pendant warm up, too, her hand still on it.

"Flor, can I ask a favor?" She reached her hands around to undo the chain of her necklace. "Will you save this for William? For when he is older? I-I'm just not sure Sully can do it. I think you will know when."

Flor understood her meaning.

"Yes, dear. It will be safe until it is time. Did Maren tell you what it was?"

"She said they represented the stars. I think, the actual junction or formation. She called it home."

CHAPTER

TWO

William turned the corner in the hall and saw Flor standing by his mother's bedside. He swallowed as his heart jumped. He recognized her from the festival. *What if she saw me taking the food?* He took a breath to clear the fear and slowly started moving toward the room. He couldn't not return to his mother's side, so he trusted it would be okay.

Flor saw him heading toward them with slow but determined steps. She gestured to Sofia to look in his direction. Of course, Sofia smiled to see her son, which quickened his step.

"Mom! How are you feeling? I saw the most amazing bird... It was tiny and so fast!"

"William, I'm so glad you're here. This is Flor. She was a friend of your grandmother's. You were right. Some people do remember her."

"Nice to meet you, ma'am." William extended his hand.

Flor smiled playfully. "Oh dear, I'm not prepared for ma'am. You have permission to call me Flor. Or we can find another name."

William shrugged, having no idea what else he could call her.

"Did I see you at our festival?"

William shifted his feet and bit his lower lip as he prepared to be in trouble.

"You left before I could talk to you. I wanted to make sure you got enough food and to check on your family."

William let out a sigh of relief. "Mom was home sick, and Dad was taking care of her. I didn't think I should be gone long."

"And you weren't sure if you were allowed to have the food."

He nodded and swallowed.

"William, forgive us for not making it clear. The food is for everyone to share. Next time we will make it clear that it is for all."

Sofia reached out and touched William's hair, resting her hand on his shoulder. "I'm the luckiest mom. Tell me about the bird—"

Sully found the bar instead of finding the flowers he went in search of. He hadn't been much of a drinking man since meeting Sofia. She had been his light, his resolve, the calm in his storm. Other than an occasional toast or celebration, he'd stayed away. But this day he left the hospital and told himself he would get some fresh air and some nice flowers for Sofia—even if he had to pick them.

He walked to use up some of the pressure-keg of energy built up by not screaming and cursing the world. The hospital was separated from the town center by a couple of blocks and a walking bridge over the creek. Sully walked quickly in search of the flowers and relief, but found none. No flowers were in view from the bridge. None that he could see down by the river.

What am I going to do, show up like a kid with a bunch of weeds? There's gotta be some decent flowers. He kept going.

Star Junction had seen many changes since Maren's time: paved roads and many families now with cars, a gas station, more new people coming in to work at the mill and lumberyard, and bars. As Sully turned the corner into the town square, Jack's Bar greeted him with an open door and sounds of the city he so missed. He started to walk by. He did. Then he heard the men laughing and cajoling, which sounded a whole lot like the relief he needed.

"A drink won't hurt. Sofia would surely understand," he said to himself. After the briefest pause, he walked through the door.

———

They had been waiting for Sully to return, though none of them said so. Sofia drifted in and out of consciousness, each time waking and looking for Sully. Each time she smiled for William and turned her eyes to Flor before drifting off again.

"Young William," Flor spoke quietly, "do you understand what is happening?"

He shrugged a little and looked down. "My mom is sick." He paused, uncertain how to say the words. "I'm afraid she won't get better." His eyes met Flor's, pleading silently with her to tell him differently.

She sat in the chair beside him. "You are a wise boy. It is okay for your heart to hurt, and it's important for you to let the hurt go through expression, like you did with the angel trumpets. We all come to this life for a limited time. Some of us have a longer time to work with. Did your grandmother ever talk to you about this?"

"Yes, she said only our bodies die, and that our souls never do. That we are always connected."

"And do you understand what she taught you? Do you believe her?"

"I-I don't know. I sometimes feel her. And sometimes talk to her in my dreams. But I still feel like I miss her because I can't talk to her out loud, or hug her, or make her laugh."

"Ahh, those are some of the best parts of loving someone." Flor patted William's hand.

"And I feel that Mom is trying so hard not to leave, but... she is. She feels like she is fading away. My father, too—in a way."

"That is a lot for a young man to carry. You are very observant, which is a gift. But sometimes, I imagine, it can feel heavier. Because you don't know what to do with it all. And you want to fix it."

"Yeah. I mean yes, I do."

"One of the important—and difficult—lessons in life is recognizing and accepting what we cannot change. And asking our hearts to guide us in compassionate action. William, it is true about your mother. She will always be with you in your heart, and she'll be able to talk to you there. That does not mean you should not feel and express grief. Your father is a different story. He will make his choices. My promise to you is that you are not alone. Your grandmother was a sister to me. That means you are family, like a nephew or grandson. My son and I are your family. I will do my best to help your father, but his choices are his own. Just as you will make yours."

William sat quietly watching his mother sleep. After replaying Flor's words in his mind and contemplating everything before him, he replied, "Maybe that is what I should call you... Grandmother Flor."

Flor patted his hand. "Okay." She smiled and whispered to him, "William, I have to go. Hug your mom. Tell her how you feel. I will check back to see that your father returned."

When she had left the room William stood up and went to his mom's bedside. He laid his head on her chest and listened to her heartbeat as his head went gently up and down with her breath. Sofia roused from her sleep enough to put her arms around William.

"I love you, Mom. I wish you could stay with me forever, but if it is time for you to go... better for you to go... then, well, you should. Because I want you to be okay. Dad is strong. I will be okay. Grandmother Flor said she will help. And you can watch it all and love us from heaven or wherever you are." Her chest was wet with his tears though he tried to hold back the sobs.

She held him as tightly as she could manage and kissed his head. "Oh, William, how I love you. You have been the light of my life—your father's, too. I know you are where you were always meant to be. You were meant to have a beautiful life, and I will be loving you throughout. Your father... be patient with him. He loves you."

They were still there when the nurse came by for her hourly check-in. William had dozed off with his mom.

Sully found his way back, bolstered by a couple or few drinks more than the originally intended one. Sofia was a saint and would surely understand. Sometimes a man just needed to be with other men. Besides, George and Vic said they could connect him to jobs. The doctors should have had time to find some hope for him, for Sofia to get better. And he would find a way to make the money back.

These thoughts coursed through his mind as he walked a bit less steadily back to the hospital. At the door to Sofia's room, he dropped the cup of waiting room coffee as he processed what was happening. William was still holding Sofia, but the doctor and nurses were also there. The doctor returned his stethoscope to hang around his neck while saying something about the time, the nurse beside him wrote on a clipboard. A second nurse had her hands on William's back, encouraging him to get up.

"Wha... What is going on?" Sully couldn't muster any other words. He pushed his way past the nurse and doctor to his wife. But Sofia's body was all that was left—peaceful, still, and cold.

"*No!*" He grabbed her shoulders and shook them. "Honey, Sofia....no, no, no!" He pushed over the IV pole and let out a scream that shook the room and echoed through the hallways as he collapsed into her body. William stared, frightened by what he saw. He reached out to hold his father, but Sully didn't feel his touch at all.

CHAPTER
THREE

E liaflore sat outside in her family's compound. A circular stone planter with simple benches around it held a beautiful and powerful angel trumpet tree, accompanied by flowers and herbs. She didn't know much about the tree other than the large trumpet flowers attracted a lot of hummingbirds, butterflies, and other beings. She didn't know why she was drawn to sit with the tree so often, but she was. She sat quietly and watched the humming-birds dance with the large flowers as she did so often in her life. Today felt different. Eliaflore felt numb to the peace that usually came in the presence of the Angel Trumpets and numb to the joy the hummingbirds shared.

Grandfather Mateo and Grandmother Analinda watched from the kitchen window, giving the child time to process the loss of her dear friend.

"Mateo, please go to her now."

Mateo looked at his wife and nodded. He kissed her on the fore-head and went to find his grieving granddaughter with the Angel

Trumpets. He quietly sat himself next to the girl and watched with her as the hummingbirds put on their show.

"Sweet Eliaflore, why do you sit here and not let the joy touch you?"

She looked up at her beloved grandfather and teacher and leaned her head on his shoulder.

"Why did Maren have to be the one to move away?"

"Child, you have known she would be going. Have you not?"

"Yes, but I... I hoped it would not be for a long time. I hoped it would not be so."

"Why, child?"

"Because she is my friend. My best friend. It feels lonely without her."

He wrapped his arms around Eliaflore and held her affectionately. "Is that why you sit without letting the joy touch you?"

She thought about his question, not sure why she felt numb to it. "I don't know why it isn't touching me," she said with furrowed brow.

He smiled kindly at her. "Granddaughter, you cannot stop one feeling without stopping them all. Let yourself feel the sadness. Release it to the trumpets. Let the emotions flow. Then you will also feel the joy the hummingbirds are sharing with you."

"But what if it never stops?"

"What if what never stops?"

"The hurt...what if it never goes away?"

"Ah, that is the illusion my love. Fear tells us that the hurt will last forever because it is so big, so much. But hurt only lasts as long as you hold it. It is okay to miss your friend. It is by releasing the tears that the illusion washes away."

"Will she ever come back?"

"Maren's path is hers to travel. She shared an important part of it with you, forging a bond not breakable by time nor distance. We cannot say whether she will be able to return here. She has many people to meet and much light and wisdom to share, her own seeds to sow. Let your connection be stronger by distance, your love and light brighter. This is the way to honor the great love you share."

"But it doesn't feel the same. I can't hug her anymore."

He squeezed her tighter, "Yes, hugs are my favorite, too."

Eliaflore let out a big sigh, tired of holding it all in. She allowed his shoulder to catch her tears, trusting that the hurt would not swallow her.

FOUR

S ully finally agreed. It had taken William weeks to convince him that the festival was for everybody and so was the food. Sully had accused him of stealing it and bringing shame. He wanted to believe his boy, but his experience of the world, especially the last few years, made him cynical. He didn't just doubt that good things existed. He suspected they were all traps, and one would have to pay dearly for believing them.

Like coming to Star Junction. This good thing cost Sofia's life, and she had been the only truly good thing in his. It was her voice in his head that made him say yes to this. Sully made them both dress up, like a Sunday function back home. Making a good impression was important. Maybe he had a sliver of hope and optimism left in him. Maybe he would meet the right person and find a job, so he and the boy could make a life here. William did his best to iron their collared shirts like he had seen his mother do so many times. Sully got cleaned up and even shaved. He glanced at the bottle of whiskey on the counter, but William intercepted.

"You ready, Dad?"

He looked at his son. "You look good, son. You did a fine job on the shirts." Sully adjusted his tie, put on his dark grey fedora, and let out a satisfied, determined breath. It was time. He put his hand on William's shoulder and guided him to the door. Today he chose possibility.

They drove past the Star Pavilion and around the block. "Dad, you okay?"

"Yeah, son. Just deciding on the best place to park. I'm still used to the big city with lots of signs and places you know are for parking!" He winked at his son, doing his best to mask his unfamiliar nerves. Nervous had never been his thing. He turned the corner, looping back toward the gathering, and parked beside the curb.

William was nervous, too. He wasn't sure which father he was getting today—the one he had grown up with who was sometimes a little too boisterous but kind hearted and good natured or the one who started taking over when his mother became ill and dominated after she died, angry, bitter, and sometimes violent.

William had found a way to blend in and get by. He found places to be invisible, like by his oak tree friend, Sir, who he couldn't help but touch with his fingertips and smile just slightly as they passed by. In his young, sometimes easily embarrassed mind, he knew his father would never fit in well without adapting. He was too "charged up." Too much city.

As they walked toward the people and the tables of food, William retucked his shirt and tried to make his Sunday pants feel less short. He felt torn between the excitement of being there at the festival, with the music and the food, and Flor... and fear. He couldn't be invisible with Sully.

Flor watched them arrive and gave a little nod to Mr. Samuels. She had hoped William would return with his father. Since William's first visit to the regular Friday gathering, they had made subtle additions to the food tables, including washable containers that could be returned to the community center or chapel any time. They hadn't thought of it before. Well, not before she watched young William putting food in his worn bag and pockets. They also had bags to fill with fresh produce and baked goods from people's homes and gardens.

Food was meant to share. Abundance grew when it grew for all. Star Junction was not a place where people were allowed to go hungry. She wouldn't have it.

As William and Sully approached the tables, Mr. Samuels said hello to William and extended his hand to Sully. "Good evening, I'm Mr. Samuels, the principal at William's school."

"Nice to meet you, Mr. Samuels. Willie says good things about the school. Hopefully he isn't causing any problems!" Sully winked, trying to be funny, but it just wasn't coming out right.

"Not at all. Young William is doing just fine. A welcome addition to our school." One of Mr. Samuels' greatest gifts was conversation. He could talk to anybody, anywhere, at any time and usually leave them at ease. This made him a very good principal.

He looked down to William and then up to meet Sully's eyes. "You have a good boy here. A fine son." He touched Sully's shoulder in a subtle pat and said, "Enjoy the fun!" as he walked away. His job was the greeting. At least, for now. He knew Flor would take over and let him know if it was time for him to do more.

William's eyes expanded as he saw how much food there was, some on wrapped plates or tied in cloth or paper along with carrying sacks with handles sewn from burlap or flour sacks. His heart truly skipped with excitement as he realized he didn't need to fill the napkins and bags he brought. Not that his dad would have let him— but maybe now they could take food home and have more than bread and thin soup.

Sully couldn't decide if he should be relieved or dubious. He never wanted to be a charity case and certainly didn't want to look like they needed to be. He had always provided for his family in the city and had never taken something for nothing before. He wasn't about to start now. Somebody must have work for him to do. He decided they could eat now and take a small amount home.

Flor waited for them at the first table with a warm smile. "Young

William, we are so glad you have joined us." She took her time with each greeting, making intentional eye contact and connection. "You must be William's father." Her words were as much an invitation as a greeting as she extended her hand.

"Dad, this is Flor—the one who knew my Grandma Maren."

"Oh, yes, um, William mentioned that. He said you were very kind to him. And my Sofia. I'm grateful for that." He paused, stumbling over all the words in the way of the ones he wanted. "Oh, um, I'm Sully, pleased to meet you, ma'am." He removed his hat with his left hand, and his eyes finally found Flor's as their hands met.

"Sir, I am very sorry for your loss."

Sully nodded as he pulled his hand back.

"Um, thank you, ma'am."

Flor handed them each a carrying sack. "Please enjoy the festival. And we don't want any of this food to go to waste. You would be helping us by taking some home. Just drop off the dishes at the community center or chapel when you are done with them."

"Well, since you put it that way, we'd be happy to help. But I'm used to working for my food."

Flor interjected before he could continue, "We can always use help setting up the festival and cleaning up afterward, especially as the weather changes and the dark comes sooner."

"I'm your man. Just tell me when to be here."

Sully and William sat on the outer edge of the festivities. They had put their food sacks in the car and filled themselves for now. The music was lively and the fire burned high. Sully wasn't quite sure what to make of it all. Back in the neighborhood, people kept to their smaller groups of activities. He'd never seen a whole town gather like this. He wished they would play some music he recognized, maybe some Bobby Darin, Frankie Avalon, or even Elvis. William really seemed to like this, though.

"Dad, do you want to walk around a bit? Maybe see what else is here. Or get dessert?" William wanted to move. He longed to get closer to the fire and the music. "Please?" He pleaded.

"Well, alright. I can always enjoy another piece of cake!" Sully replied as he winked and patted his belly. He was feeling a little bolder now, perhaps from the good food or the time away from his thoughts.

They stood up and walked toward the tables, William leading them through the center of people. The crowd was friendly and welcoming, and Sully found himself lulled into a sense of enjoyment, brandishing his first true smile since arriving.

As they approached the dessert table, Sully found his voice, the big city one that William was worried about. "My, my, my, don't these all look delicious!" His hands talked with him, fanning over the spread of sweets. "Mmm-mmm-mmm. You ladies have outdone yourselves, and I, for one, am happier for it." He winked and tipped his hat.

Flor passed behind the women at the table and responded, "We are glad you are enjoying yourself."

"Oh, yes, we are. Haven't had food this good since leaving home. I am much obliged."

"Mom!" a boy about William's age called out from a distance.

Flor watched Edward heading toward them from the fire. She had a plate ready for him, knowing he would be hungry after playing music and working the fire. She held the plate up so he could see. Sully and William turned to see who was coming and moved to the left to open the path. William moved a little farther back when he recognized Edward from school, feeling uneasy and trying to go unnoticed.

Edward's focus was on the food and his mother. If he noticed William, he didn't show it as he walked past and up to his waiting food.

Flor greeted him with a smile and praise as she looked at him. "Aah, I see you played fully and well."

"Thank you, Mom. It was amazing. I'm starving!"

She laughed. Edward was often ravenous lately, going through a growth spurt. His appetite seemed to double with every inch of height.

"Edward, do you know William? I believe he is one of your class-mates... William, Sully, this is my son Edward."

Edward glanced over to William without enthusiasm but with trained politeness. "Yeah... Hey." Was the extent of the greeting he could manage between bites.

"Ha! We're interfering with your meal. You're a fine boy, Eddie. Yep, a fine young man. I can tell." Sully was full of praise. "Willie would be wise to learn from you."

William shrank a little more each time Sully spoke to Edward, but Edward seemed enthralled.

"Nice to meet you, sir."

"It's our pleasure, Eddie. Yep. You and Willie will make great friends. He's smart, ya' know. The kind of smart you want on your side. And notices everything." Sully had a way of being bigger than life—from his polished shoes to his tie and hat. He could capture an audience and tell them what they wanted to hear.

William watched the exchange between his father and Edward, glancing at Flor briefly in between.

"Son, let's find a place for you to sit and eat comfortably." Flor led Edward away, and William was grateful. She turned and added, "Gentlemen, thank you again for joining us tonight. Please let us see you every week."

Flor and Edward found a spot under one of the guardian trees, not that the boy had waited to eat. His plate held just a portion of what it had started with.

"Mom, thank you for the plate of food. It is perfect after the fire."

"I'm glad I chose well for you." She smiled at him playfully, knowing he would have devoured anything she put on that plate. "You did a wonderful job tonight, Edward. Your gift was well-received."

He paused his bites for a moment. "It all felt very strong tonight. It was cool."

"I noticed you avoided your classmate. Why is that?"

He shrugged. "I don't know. I don't like him. He's different."

"Really?" Flor was intrigued by this. She knew her son well and suspected what his challenges would be.

"Yes." Edward was matter-of-fact and his tone convinced. He took a few more bites before he realized his mother was inviting him deeper. "But his dad seems cool. He should be more like his dad." He hoped to save himself.

"Interesting. Tell me more." This was Flor's shorthand for: "What did you see, notice, observe, feel? And what do you think it means?"

"I saw that he dresses well. He is a man of the world. He has a keen eye. And he's friendly. I like that he called me Eddie." Edward tried to sound mature.

"But your name is Edward."

"Yeah, but that's what people do, you know. Cool people have nicknames. They shorten names to something cooler."

"I see. And the nickname didn't feel different to you?"

"Yeah, it did! It felt bigger."

Flor remained silent and let Edward finish his food. The festival was winding down. She watched as the townspeople began to clean up and say good night to their neighbors. She watched William still alone with his father, who was trying to feel as big as he seemed to Edward.

"Son, William is new in town and just lost his mother. He is the grandchild of one of my dearest friends, a sister to me when I was even younger than you. He is learning to adjust the best he can. I have seen that you two will be like brothers one day. Perhaps that will start with you just being a good neighbor. Or as friendly as you believe his father to be."

"But, Mom—"

She met his objection with a look and a slight wave of her index finger pointed at the sky.

"Perhaps."

CHAPTER

FIVE

Twenty-Eight Years Before

E liaflore was a quiet, thoughtful girl who lived with an open heart for all. She was being raised by Grandfather Mateo and Grandmother Analinda. When they adopted her, they were already considered elders in the community. But when they laid eyes on her, Analinda beamed with recognition and delight. "She has arrived!"

Eliaflore had shown a great capacity for love—clear, unfiltered, unwavering love—from before she could walk. Her grandparents had been teachers of many over the years, so teaching her came with great ease. Her understanding of connection originated from birth. She learned to work with energy in many ways—discernment, filtering, and transmutation—before she fully had the words to identify the energy or the process.

By the time she was four, Mateo and Analinda saw that she came from such pure love that she did not recognize when others did not —a blind spot from a very early age. She operated under the assumption that everybody saw as she did, felt as she did, and understood as she did. This, her grandparents knew, would be her challenge.

For the first time in its history Star Junction had received an influx of migrant workers from all over. The railroad brought them to Exton. The mill attracted them to Star Junction. Most came for a season on their way to brighter dreams and the hope of bigger opportunities. A few felt at home and stayed longer, getting to know the townspeople and the town herself. Many of these were young men who took a fancy to the girls.

The town was not prepared for this. While the people weren't naive exactly, they did have an innocence about them. Perhaps more so than those of a larger city. They hadn't thought to teach the girls about being savvy and recognizing the motives of a male suitor. Over the course of five years, there were a rash of unplanned pregnancies, and a handful of young girls left by their suitors to fend for themselves. Maren's older sister had been one of these. Most stayed with their families and raised their child within the family unit. Two fell into clouds of shame their families couldn't free them from. They fled town in secret, and left their babies to be raised by others. One young mother did not survive childbirth. Her family—filled with grief and heartache, and other children—made the difficult decision to have her child raised by beloved elders.

Star Junction still had many elders to teach the younger generations and guide the townspeople. Most families thrived. Maren's family had been here for generations. Both she and Eliaflore were raised to be teachers, keepers of the star path. All children in Star Junction were taught the ways of the path keepers. The ways of connection and harmony. Some were destined to go out into the world to plant seeds and grow roots and do their part to share wisdom and light. Others would ultimately make their life in Star Junction, to teach the next teachers and path keepers. Eliaflore was destined to be a leader for those that stayed. As one of the youngest of this generation she only remembered the few who had left in her lifetime with vague familiarity, more as if she had met them in a dream.

Maren was the first to leave that she knew well and loved so deeply. They both loved without reserve and sometimes blindly. With Maren now far away, Eliaflore spent much of her time over the last few years with Ikenial. He was a little more than two years older, but she kept up with him in all ways but size.

Eliaflore was one of the three children left to be raised by elders. The other two were: Ikenial, who was older, and Rygg who was younger. To Flor, Rygg felt like the mountain and the trees—deep-rooted sentient, reliable, strong. Rygg kept to himself. He was comfortable in nature. Comfortable not speaking. As they got a little older, he would discover an affinity for sports and leadership.

Ikenial felt connected to nothing, except, perhaps Eliaflore. These three shared the experience of being raised by community elders or others not willing to allow a child to go unloved. While Eliaflore was close with many of the other children, both older and younger, Ikenial was her partner in play. In her innocence, she couldn't interpret his differing views and temperamental nature. His darker views seeped in and conflicted with hers.

Now, nine-year old Eliaflore sat at the fire with Mateo and Analinda. This was not the monthly talking fire with the larger group. It was just for them in their courtyard. The grandparents sat patiently with the normally energetic and joyful nine-year-old.

"Eliaflore, dear, would you like more cocoa?"

"No, thank you, Grandmother."

"What has captured your thoughts?"

The young girl stopped staring at the fire and looked at her beloved guardians. "Where do I come from? I mean, who are my parents?"

Mateo answered, "We have told you the story before. Have we not?"

"Yes, but there must be more. I'm so glad you two adopted me. I love my life. I just wonder."

"Sweet child, we are happy to talk about this as often as you wish. I have a question for you, though. What has put the question in your mind?"

"Ikenial says his family is not really his, and he has no ties to them."

"Family does not have to be blood to have ties. We simply choose to love."

"Yes, but what if. I don't know. What if something is missing?"

"Like what?"

"Ikenial says that he can feel that they are not his real family and that he does not belong. It makes me sad."

"And makes you question."

"Can it be? What if our real, I mean, the people who..." She sighed, not sure how to word the question without hurting those who chose to raise her.

"What if your birth parents what?"

"What if they are missing me? Would they be? Would his parents be missing him? Would he feel like he belonged if he were with them...or would it be worse?"

"Those are all very big questions for a young girl," Analinda said kindly.

"And very good questions for us to look at," Mateo added. Eliaflore was mature enough to have the questions, which meant it was time to address them. "We've told you there was a time when some of the young women of our town, some of them teenagers, were courted by men who were passing through for work—either working at the mill or the quarry toward Exton. Some of the suitors were fine young men who chose to stay and start a family. And as is sometimes the way of things, some were not. It was a difficult time for our community. Some of the girls felt shame and left. Their loss was felt deeply. Some stayed long enough to give birth. One did not survive childbirth—your mother. We do not know who all of the young men were, but it is safe to say that those who abandoned the one they turned into a mother would not have been equipped for the fatherhood they ran from. It is not for us to tell the stories. We do know that your mother was a beautiful spirit. She was loving and joyful and very naive in the ways of the world, especially the one outside of Star Junction." He paused to let her take it in. "We also know we are all where we are meant to be. It is by no accident or mistake that you are with us. It is not our job to question what is. It is our job to live it." Mateo spoke with deep reverence.

"Our birth parents are the means by which we arrive. We should always have love and gratitude for them and that gift. Some experience great pain to provide the gift and even sacrifice but it is all by agreement. Ikenial was always meant to be with his family as you were meant to be with us," Analinda added.

"Thank you, Grandmother and Grandfather. Sometimes I forget that part." Eliaflore smiled, relieved at the reminder for her heart. "Can I have more cocoa now?"

CHAPTER
SIX

In the year that William and Sully had been alone, Flor had made good on her promise to Sofia. She made sure to check in on William weekly, and Mr. Samuels knew to let her know if he saw any problems. When he informed her that William's clothes were ill-fitting and tattered—William had grown out of his and was borrowing from his father, who was much taller—Flor arranged a clothing swap at the Friday fire. All of the clothes that were left would be made available at the community center.

Despite Flor's encouragement for Edward to befriend William, it hadn't happened. William kept to himself, usually going home after school to check on his father. His only stops included the library, Sir, and the cluster of trees before his house. He liked to listen and watch before going inside, sometimes delaying if he heard his father's voice.

Flor was aware of William's patterns and her son's inaction. She felt it was time to take a different approach. Flor and Edward sat for breakfast and talked.

"How has it been going with William?"

Edward looked down at his food and shrugged. He wished she

would drop it already. She watched him intently, waiting for her answer.

"I told you before. I don't like him. I don't know why you want me to."

"It is not what I want. It is what I see."

"Well, I don't. He is not so great, you know. He's always fighting, and I've seen him steal. Why would you want me to be friends with someone like that?" Edward made it sound worse. He hadn't ever seen him steal, but a classmate bully accused him of doing so. Edward knew when he said the words that they were a mistake. Flor saw through him.

"Maybe a friend is what he needs."

"I don't think he wants friends."

"You don't think?"

"No, you taught me to pay attention, to notice how people behave. I think he is no good."

"I taught you to look with your heart. Not your eyes or your judgment."

Edward was frustrated. He didn't know why, but things had changed since William had come to town.

"Son, I am not asking you to spend every minute with him. I am asking you to get to know him, to open your heart, and to show kindness to a neighbor and classmate."

Edward couldn't say anything else. He would try to be nice, but she couldn't make him like it.

Edward entered Mrs. Peterson's sixth grade classroom. He normally sat near the middle or back, but he saw William sitting in the first row by the window. Edward knew the seat next to William was usually empty so he changed course, moved the seat slightly away, and sat.

"Hey."

William nodded, not sure what to make of it. Edward had barely said anything to him in over a year. Should he be friendly or on guard? He went back to watching the birds until Mrs. Peterson began class.

William worked hard. For a few months he was able to coerce Sully into showing up to the Friday gatherings. Sully tried for a while. He'd help set up and clean up enough that he felt he earned the food they took. In front of townspeople, he would rally and put on a friendly show. In the beginning, he would even show up sober.

Sully had found work at the lumberyard for a few months before the mill shut down followed by odd jobs. But he was losing the war against the anger that raged inside him and the fear when he looked at his son. He couldn't help it. William had his mother's auburn hair and green eyes. The sight of the boy only hurt, only reminded Sully of Sofia, of everything that had changed, and of being an ill-equipped fish out of water in a place he didn't want to be. *Willie deserves better,* he would say to himself as he took another drink. Eventually, he only went to town to buy more alcohol.

William did his best to look after his father and himself.

"Pop, I brought back some food from the festival. You should eat something."

"Don't tell me what to do, son. I didn't work for that food. I won't eat it."

"Please, Pop... I'm worried about you. I worked for it. I set up chairs and tables. I helped so we could—"

Sully slapped him.

"I said stop!"

They stood stunned, frozen in a moment they both wish hadn't happened, but Sully could never undo. He snapped out of it and moved to pull his son to him. "Oh Willie, oh no... I don't know what happened. I'm sorry boy. Please, you're okay. I know you're just trying to take care of your old man."

It was the first time Sully had held his son since Sofia died and the first time he'd directly hit him. Sully cried as he tried to undo the slap, gently patting his son's head, shoulders, and back as William wrapped his arms around him, and cried into his chest.

This was how it started. Months spent isolated in a shack with bottle after bottle drowned Sully's thoughts and drove away his being. By the time William was twelve, he had learned to fish in the river and hunt small animals. He tried to have a chicken for eggs, but it was killed by a coyote. He'd actually tried to bring it in at night, but Sully wouldn't have it. Flor gifted him the chicken at one of their weekly check-ins. When she learned that the chicken was lost to the predator, she offered a new solution. "Young William, if you come to help me clean the chicken coop each week, your share of the eggs will be plenty for you and your father. And when it is time, there will be chicken for you as well."

"Thank you, Grandmother Flor." He wanted to say more. She felt it.

"What is it, William? More words are on your tongue."

"I can't get my father to eat. He just won't. He—"

"I see. I am sorry to hear this, Young William. It is much for you to go through. I will check on him. He will not know why." She rested her hand on William's back in reassurance.

Flor found a reason to visit the remote home and made sure it was during the day when the boy was at school. She noted the makeshift garden William had planted, the clothesline tied between an oak tree and the house, and a very large wood pile. The Nomad station wagon looked like it hadn't been moved in some time. The house was barely still intact and she wondered how they came to this property, not imagining who would have sold it in this condition. These dwellings had all been left long ago. She closed her eyes, thanking the trees for protecting the boy and the wood for its sacrifice. She could detect signs of William's light outside, but the heaviness surrounding the home was immense.

The knock startled Sully. They didn't get visitors. Nobody knocked. Even his liquor deliveries were just left on the porch. He figured he imagined it until it happened again. Tap, tap, tap.

"Alright, hang on!" he grumbled as he made his way to the door. He opened it just about six inches—enough to look through but not enough for whoever was there to get a view of the state of things. He was startled to see Flor there waiting.

"Oh, uh, ma'am. I-I didn't know it was you. Excuse me. I wasn't expecting anyone."

Flor just looked at him kindly as he bowed his head.

"Good morning, Sully. We have missed you on Fridays."

"Oh, yes, ma'am. I haven't been feeling much up to it of late. My boy says he's been helping out, though. Not just taking food without earning it."

"William has been of great help. He works hard, indeed."

Sully still stood behind the door, reluctant to let her see.

"Sully, I'd like to sit with you for a bit with your permission. I suspected you weren't feeling well, so I brought some special tea to help your stomach and maybe clear your head a bit."

"That's very kind of you. I guess that would be all right. Haven't had a visitor here before."

Flor waited patiently outside the door until Sully realized it was his move. He couldn't decide between going out to her or allowing her to come in.

"I know how hard it can be to keep the house up when we aren't feeling well," she offered to help his decision.

He stepped back and allowed the door to open. "Please, won't you come in?" Sully was unsteady on his feet, not from fresh drinking but more a cumulative effect and deterioration of his body.

Flor helped him to the couch. "Sit. It's okay. I will find you a mug for the tea." She had already spotted one in the kitchen sink. There was no separation between the kitchen and living space, other than a small counter. She quickly washed the mug and poured the herbal concoction sweetened with honey. As she handed him the mug, she smiled. "With your permission, I'd like to sit."

"Of course, my apologies. I've forgotten my manners."

"Not at all. Please, drink the tea. Slowly."

As Sully took a few sips, tentatively at first, she took in the room. She could feel that Sofia was still there. Likely for William. She suspected that William tried to keep the place up. There was enough order and the trash wasn't overflowing. She sat in silence with Sully for as long as he could stand it, giving the tea time to help his discomfort. She finally broke the silence for him.

"How is the tea feeling for you?

"Um, it's just fine. Tasted a little weird at first. I'm not gonna lie. But it's soothing, I think."

She smiled. "Good." Despite his fidgeting, Flor found his eyes and held his gaze. She saw so much pain in them. "Sully, dear, are you okay?" She knew he wasn't, but she needed to ask while their eyes were locked. It was too much for him to shoulder, and he began to sob.

"I-I don't know who I am anymore without Sofia. She was my life. My poor boy... he's such a good boy. He doesn't deserve what I'm putting him through. I hurt my boy. What is wrong with me?"

"William is a good boy. And he loves you."

"He shouldn't."

"Nonsense. You are his father. Good or bad, mistakes and all, you are his father."

"For twelve years I had Sofia. She didn't like me drinking so I didn't. A sip here and there. That was all. I never wanted to disappoint her. Now, it's all I want to do—drink until I die and can be with her." Sully startled himself with that declaration. "I don't know why I'm telling you this. I'm sorry, ma'am. That's too much. I shouldn't have."

"Nonsense. We are two adults having an honest conversation. I will be as honest with you. You are not just choosing to die. You are choosing to destroy. It is a very painful and destructive path to death. Why do you wish to punish yourself so? And your son?"

"I don't know how to be here. We never should have left the city."

"If you hadn't left, your wife would not have made it here in time. And William would not have made it here at all. He would be stuck in the city without solace. It would likely have been far rougher for him."

"But we had people there...friends we could rely on."

"Forgive me, Sully. Of course we need community. I am truly sorry that we have failed you in that way. It would have been better if you had moved into town and not so far removed. This could still help. I can arrange a house for you in town. If you choose to heal and make things better."

Sully didn't respond. He didn't know how. He had been stuck in anger and resentful of life itself. Nothing seemed possible. They had spent their money on this house. He didn't stay employed long enough to earn much. It hadn't occurred to him that change could be possible. Despite some motions to the contrary, he gave up the second he saw Sofia dead in the hospital bed. He never would forgive himself for not being there and for not being able to save her.

"How did you find this house? I'm curious."

"A buddy found a contact in Phoenix, who found the listing in the paper and put us in touch with the seller. He said this was the best we could afford for our budget. He seemed like a nice guy. Said he was from here and knew the area well. He said the hillside proper-ties were premium because of the privacy and view."

Flor felt ill in a quick wave. She didn't want to believe what she suspected. She would verify and work to put a stop to any future unscrupulous sales.

"Ma'am, I'm feeling quite a bit better. That tea is really some-thing. Look, I know you mean well. I'm grateful you care about my son and this town. I'm gonna try. No, I'm going to make things better. But, ma'am, if I am too late... if something should happen to me... will you still, I mean, will you look after my boy? I believe he would be in good hands with you and your boy."

"I made a promise to your wife that I will also make to you. If something happens to you, I will take William in. He is family as Maren was family. He will be well cared for and loved. However, he would much prefer to be with his father. If you decide you wish to move into town, I will find a place for you. No additional cost. It will be a straight swap. Please take care, Sully. I'll send more tea for you."

When William came home, Sully was showered, clean shaven, and had done laundry. It lasted a few days. Until the next case of liquor got dropped off.

Edward ran hot and cold with William. William was too quiet, too angry, too weird. He should be more like his dad—friendly and outgoing. Instead, he was rude. He barely responded to people when they talked to him. Never mind that some of those people were kids who were commenting on William's ill-fitting clothes and his ever-growing reddish hair. He hadn't had a real cut since his mother died. William was Edward's blind spot.

Since he crawled, Edward had been taught to see with his heart, to be open and not to judge, to connect in and remain neutral. But that seemed a lot easier when he was younger. By the time William had moved to town, Edward was firmly planted in his limited perception. He had known all the same people his whole life. Very few new people had come to Star Junction and none in his grade. When William arrived and was so different, that's all Edward could see. That and the fact that William had a dad who seemed cool and charming. That made him lucky. Edward resented him without even knowing it. And was more than a little jealous when Flor took an interest in William.

At the same time, Edward tried to honor his mother's wishes. He was a good son, but he was starting to reach the age when he thought he knew better than she. And that made it difficult to listen to her. So he half-heartedly attempted to engage with William from time to time at school though not always with great timing. He often had only limited success.

William was already weary. He'd lost his mother. He was losing his father. Kids were tormenting him. All he wanted was peace and some normalcy. He wanted regular meals and to sleep through the nights without hearing his father fall over drunk, breaking furniture, or cursing life. When Edward started approaching him, he just didn't trust it.

With just a month left in the school year, fate intervened in the form of their teacher, Mrs. Peterson. She teamed them up on an end-of-year project that included researching a topic, doing a presentation, and creating artwork or a visual display that they included in the presentation. Edward didn't like doing research. William didn't like the idea of doing a presentation in front of the class. Both were okay with creating the visual display.

They had a week to do the project but avoided it for the first few days. This left them with the weekend to do the project and have it ready for Monday. Friday afternoon they sat at one of the school's picnic tables to decide what to do.

"Maybe we can talk to your mom. She might have an idea for us or good information to get us started," William tried.

"No."

"Why not?"

"Because she's my mom. Besides, everybody's going to do something about Star Junction. We should think of something else. We could go to your dad, instead."

"We can't." He knew he said it too quickly.

"Why not?" Edward's voice was irritated.

William fumbled for an answer. "My dad's sick. He can't help us."

"Well, what about you? You're from somewhere else. You must know of something interesting that isn't here."

"Well, where I'm from has lots of really tall buildings, lots of cars —compared to here—and I got to go to the ocean."

"No way, you never saw the ocean."

"Of course I did. The Atlantic. We visited it one last time before we left for here."

"Wow. What's it like? And how long did it take you to drive here? The Atlantic is so far."

"Yeah. It took us days. Maybe a week. The ocean is beautiful and powerful. During big storms, the waves can destroy houses and roads even. Where we went had big sandy beaches and lots of seashells."

"Do you have any? Maybe we should do our presentation on the Atlantic or your trip." Edward didn't know why he thought it, but it occurred to him that if people knew more about William's story, they might accept him more.

"I think I still have some. I can check when I get home."

"I could go with you if you want to keep working on this."

"No... you can't." William again said it too quickly. The thought of anyone seeing his house and his father terrified him. He quickly tried to smooth out the panic in his tone. "Remember, my dad is sick. It wouldn't be good for you to go."

"We can meet back here."

"Probably not today. I've got chores. I can work on it tomorrow, though. You can find a book at the library about the Atlantic. You know, so we could get some facts about it for the presentation. I'm sure the librarian, Ida, will find a good one for us."

Edward wasn't thrilled with the idea. He only went into the library when the whole class went. "Yea, okay. I can get a book. But we'll go through it together."

William nodded in agreement. He looked off in the direction of home and picked up his books and bag. "I've gotta go. See you tomorrow."

"Be here at ten."

But William wasn't there at ten. He wasn't there at eleven, either. Edward went home convinced, again, of his lack of character. Flor found Edward carving.

"How is your project coming?"

"It isn't. He didn't show. I told you, he's no good."

"Really? So, are you working on the project now?"

"What am I supposed to do by myself?"

"Contribute. Do the parts you can with the book you brought home."

"But we're supposed to do that together."

"I see. Have you considered the possibility that something has happened that could be interfering with William being on time?"

"Why do you always try to defend him? You're not listening to what I tell you."

"Son, you will one day be wise beyond your years. But you still have much to learn. I will ask you one question. Which eyes are you looking through?"

Edward steamed. He couldn't focus on the carving and didn't want to read the book. *Fine.* He thought. *I will go to him. Then maybe she will believe me.*

He knew where to go but hadn't ever spent much time on this part of the mountain. These old shacks had all been abandoned long ago, and they felt kind of dreary to him. The book was heavier on his back than he realized it would be, which only made him more determined to catch William being irresponsible.

Edward tried to stay on dirt and rocks when he got closer. The grasses were brown now and crunched under his feet. He felt like a spy or a detective, like in one of the books he enjoyed. He cast himself as the hero—the one who would discover the evil wrongdoings and save the town. Or at least himself.

He passed a couple of former homes that had long-since been reclaimed by nature, and his mood began to shift. His mind quieted and his walk slowed. *Does he really live out here?* He saw what must be William's house up ahead—the only one with a car out front—and moved into the brush and wooded area. He wanted to see but not be seen. He found a spot behind a cluster of well-placed trees just in time. The shouting from the house startled him.

"Don't lie to me, boy!"

"But, Pop, I have homework. Really. I'm supposed to meet Edward to do this project together."

"I told you; I won't stand for lies. Your mother would be devastated to know you're a little lying bastard!"

Edward could hear commotion. It sounded like hitting and furniture being shoved around. Something smashed.

"Dad, stop! Please!" William cried. "I'm not lying." He burst through the door, Sully following him with looped belt in hand.

William just had to get out the door, out to the trees. Sully wouldn't be able to follow. William jumped down the steps to get away as Sully swung the belt. Sully lost his balance and stumbled down the two steps.

"God damn, you little bastard! It just ain't right."

Edward watched in horror. He had never witnessed violence like that. He didn't know what to do—whether to jump in or run away. He remained invisible, paralyzed in silence.

All got silent. William froze not ten feet from where Sully lay, waiting to see if it was safe to help his father up. They all remained suspended in this moment, not knowing if it was time to run or return. Sully rolled to his knees and started sobbing.

"Oh, Willie boy, I'm sorry. I-I don't know what happens." He struggled to get to his feet but fell and leaned instead against the wall. William recognized the moment and went to his father to help him inside.

"Dad, are you okay?" He did his best at half Sully's size to help his father up the stairs and into the house.

"Thank you, son... I just need to rest. You're a good boy."

William came back out and put his head in his hands trying desperately to suppress a scream. He had cuts on his lip and above his eye but didn't realize it until he brought his hands down. Holding down the sobs, he grabbed the axe and started chopping wood. The woodpile was already more than they would likely use in the winter, but it wasn't about that. He just chopped, every blow a reclamation of self, every swing an expression of rage and defiance at what had happened.

No, I do not submit. No, this will not be life. No, I am not bad, not a liar, not a thief. He chopped until the roar had left, and he sank to the ground and rested against the tree behind him.

Edward wiped tears from his eyes. He waited until William went back inside and then headed home. He didn't want William to know he saw him. It was enough that William had to endure it. He shouldn't have to know he'd been seen.

When Edward arrived home, he found Flor in the garden. She stood to meet him, and he cried openly. Flor wrapped her arms around her son.

"I'm sorry, Mom."

"I am glad you have found your right eyes. But now you have seen something that is hard for a heart to see."

"Yes. I'm sorry I judged him without knowing his story. I was wrong about his father."

"Perhaps."

"I don't know how a man, a father, can treat his son like that."

"Sully has lost himself. You saw what he wanted us to see, the him he tried to be before they arrived here. You were not wrong; you just did not see beyond that version of him. You did not look to his whole being."

"What do we do?"

"We continue to offer support and friendship. We check in often. Provide safe places for William and have compassion for a soul soon departing from a painful path."

"You mean he is going to die?"

"It is what I see, but I do not know when. We can only help William as much as we are able."

Edward thought about this. "I'm going to go work on our report."

CHAPTER
SEVEN

William arrived sometime after 1:00 p.m. He had waited until Sully was asleep, grabbed his bag with the shells and some pictures, and headed to Flor and Edward's house. He had never come through the front patio before. Flor usually had him come through the back to the chicken coops. He walked through the patio and was mesmerized by all the aromas and flowers. It was so enchanting, he almost forgot to knock on the door.

Flor opened the door with a warm smile.

"What a nice surprise, young William. What brings you here?"

"Um, I was supposed to meet Edward earlier, but, I... um... couldn't make it. I was hoping he'd want to work on the project now."

"Please come in." Flor led him to the large kitchen table. He wasn't sure what she was cooking, but it smelled like the best thing he'd ever smelled. "Are you hungry?"

William's eyes lit up. "Yes, ma'am."

"There's that ma'am again," she teased. "Please sit. I'll get Edward and make you some lunch."

Edward came in with the book and the work he'd done so far. "Hey."

"Edward, I'm sorry I'm late. Really."

Edward tried not to be distracted by the swollen lip and cut on William's eyebrow. He shrugged and answered as lightly as he could.

"It's okay. I'm just glad you're here now. I got started for us."

"I found some of the shells and a couple of pictures." William opened his bag and pulled out two scallop shells, a clam shell, a large whelk, and small jingle shells.

"Whoa, those are amazing. Did you really find them yourself?"

"Yeah, my mom and I used to look for shells together. We only got to go a few times. These are from the last visit."

Edward picked up the pictures. "What are these?"

"Well, the top one is a picture of our favorite beach. The next one is of me, my mom, and grandma. Grandma is holding a huge whelk shell. I don't know what happened to it."

Flor was listening as she prepared their food. She brought over a bowl of stew and fresh bread.

"May I see the picture?" she asked William, though Edward was holding it.

"Yeah, sure." Edward handed her the photograph. She took the longest breath William had ever heard. He watched her close her eyes for a minute, as if saving a copy of the photograph in her mind.

"Thank you. It is a gift to see a picture of my dear friend and sister after so much time."

Edward wasn't sure if she had told him before. She handed the photo back to him, and he looked closely at Maren.

"Mom, she looks like you."

Flor smiled at the thought. "We have always felt as close as sisters. Perhaps that is why."

"You really do. You kind of remind me of her, too," William added.

"That is a beautiful compliment."

The boys worked on their project for the next few hours, each taking turns writing the paper and creating a display of the shells with descriptions of the beings that once lived inside. Edward agreed that he would keep them there and take them to school on Monday.

Before sending William home with tea for his father, Flor also gave him a salve for his cut lip and eyebrow. "William, please listen to me. You are welcome here. If there is a time when you need to leave your house, if just for a time, to feel safe when your father is not himself, come here. Do not let him hit you anymore. You are fast and sure on your feet. Leave and come here. Do you understand?"

They both knew Sully wasn't capable of following William. The boy could get away but felt he needed to try and make his father better. To convince him that he was confused.

William took a deep breath in and gave Flor a quick hug.

Monday morning Edward took all the parts of the presentation to the classroom. The plan was that they would arrive a few minutes early to set up the display. Mrs. Peterson agreed to let them in and make a space on one of the classroom counters under the window. Edward went ahead and got everything ready. By the time class began, William still hadn't arrived. Edward kept looking at the empty desk, wrestling with an uneasy feeling in his gut. At the first break he approached Mrs. Peterson.

"Edward, are you okay?"

"Yes, ma'am, but I'm worried for William. I have to go check on him. I know he wouldn't miss our presentation."

"Well, we can postpone it until tomorrow. I'm sure he'll be fine."

"No, I'm sorry. I need find him. I think he needs help." Edward didn't wait for her to respond, instead running toward home to get his mother.

When he got home, he found Flor in prayer at the angel trumpets. "Mom! Mom, I think William is in trouble."

"What is it, Edward? Why do you think that?"

"He didn't come to school today. After what happened the other day... I just, I think we need to go check on him."

"Yes, I agree." Flor got up and retrieved some supplies and her healing bag.

The mother and son walked briskly, sometimes jogging, to get to William's house. Flor slowed them both as they approached. "Son, slow down. Please take a deep breath and connect again to the earth and your heart. We must be aware of what we are entering."

Edward didn't want to slow down. His heart was racing, the adrenaline coursing through him. But he obeyed, taking a long slow breath in and feeling his feet on the earth. When he had calmed slightly, he nodded to her that he was ready, and they continued.

They saw from a distance that the door was ajar, but all was silent. Flor put her hand on Edward's shoulder, "Please wait for me here."

She went inside and found Sully on the ground, face down. A thin blanket covered him without concealing his awkwardly contorted body. She didn't need to check, but she knelt down anyway and felt for a pulse. He was cold and gray. She closed her eyes for a moment and then stood.

"Mom... is he dead?" She looked at her son standing in the doorway.

"Yes, Sully has left this life."

"But where's William?"

"He is with the Mountain."

"How do we find him?"

"The Mountain and the Watcher will lead us to him when it is time."

William had arrived home on Saturday to find Sully still sleeping. He quietly put the tea and stew that Flor had sent into the refrigerator, cleaned as much as he could without making noise, and then went to bed to read. Sunday morning William convinced Sully to take a shower and have some of Grandmother's tea. Sully was weak, but

William was able to help him into the shower. Afterward, they sat on the couch, and William read aloud from his book. The energy was unusually calm but felt better than the days he had become accustomed to.

"Son, you're a good boy. Your mama would be proud. I'm proud. I'm sorry you got me as a father... You always deserved better than I could give."

"Dad, I love you. *You.*" He said it a second time for emphasis, hoping his father could feel the truth of it.

"I love you, too. I just ain't very good at it. Your mom made me good. I miss her."

William had a knot building in the pit of his stomach. The words should have made him feel good, but he knew something was very, very wrong.

"I know. Me too..." *And you,* he thought. *Please don't go.*

Sully drifted to sleep, and William did laundry, doing his best to wring out the soap and the water with his still small hands. He tried to keep the fear and emotions from taking over, repeating in his head over and over: *Please don't go. Please. I love you.*

But when he came back in from hanging the clothes on the line and collecting firewood, he found Sully getting up and bowled over in pain.

"Dad! Are you okay?" He ran to help his father.

Sully cried out in pain and fell to the ground. William tried to get him up, tried to hold him, but he just wasn't strong enough to carry the full weight of his father. Sully crashed to the floor. "Dad, no, please don't go! Please!"

William kneeled next to his father and tried to help, tried to rouse him, but he was gone. William grabbed the blanket, covered Sully to his shoulders, and lay next to him sobbing. It was all he knew to do, all he could think of until sometime in the night.

William had the thought that he needed to be outside—to walk, to run, to breathe, and maybe to scream. He grabbed his jacket, the flashlight he got for his fifth birthday, and his dad's hat before going out into the night.

The sounds of night were different. Hiking alone in the dark without direction, wandering, just short of lost, had a way of focusing attention. William walked and climbed, trying to outrun his thoughts and outwit the emotions he couldn't seem to contain. But only the sounds helped: the hoo-hoo of an unseen owl, twigs snapping and leaves swishing from invisible creatures, a screech in the distance, something running, perhaps.

Birds had different songs than those in the daytime. Bats chirped and swished in the air as they caught tiny insects overhead. Since his mom died, William had snuck out at night often to sit under the trees and try to feel okay while Sully became unrecognizable with drink and despair. He didn't know where he was going or why. He just knew he had to go. Had to be outside. Had to be on the mountain. Had to listen to the sounds and be under the stars.

The stars and moon provided enough light to see the pathways —the openings between rocks, bushes, and clusters of trees. Still, William clenched his unlit flashlight in his right hand, ready to light as much as a small, child's flashlight could. He didn't know why he brought it, but it was all he could think of in his rush to get out—a gift from seven years prior, a promise of adventure from his parents. Part of a boy's adventure kit, sure to excite any young boy raised in a city of high rises and street lights.

He was determined to use it now. To say, "Look, Mom, it matters. It works." Perhaps that could bring her back and the father that Sully was then, the one who doted on his family and brimmed with pride over his beautiful wife and good, smart son. Back when he felt he had a purpose and a drive to show off. William had taken good care of the flashlight, making sure the batteries were good and not corroded.

For hours William followed what seemed like a path until he couldn't anymore. He just couldn't find it with the light from the sky obscured. He could only see boulders, bushes, trees, and darkness.

He turned on the flashlight that had been his hope for so long, that he had been so careful with, but its light wasn't enough to see more than a few inches from him.

"Aagh!" he screamed and hurled the flashlight against the boulders before dropping to the ground and sobbing as he pounded the earth with his fists.

The earth held him and received his pain. Eventually, William slept, unknowingly surrounded and protected.

In the morning, as the day came alive, the sounds did too. Birds sang, telling stories. Squirrels and other critters scurried for their morning snacks. William woke with the noise and the sunlight. He sat up slowly and stretched out, his body stiff as his eyes took in the surroundings.

He was in a partial enclosure or cave, which explained why he couldn't see. Boulders lined one side and were backed by trees, but the other side was the mountain herself. His smashed flashlight lay at the base of the boulders, the batteries spilled out. *I'm sorry. I didn't mean it.*

He picked up the pieces and batteries and put them in his pocket. William ran his hands along the boulders and the wall of the mountain. "Thank you for keeping me safe."

He headed toward the path he had entered on and couldn't help but see the large paw prints. *They could have been there before. Right?*

He only now thought about water. He was thirsty, hungry, and had no idea where he was. He tried to remember what his grandmother Maren had taught him about the mountains and Star Junction. It all seemed like magical, made-up stories to a boy raised in the city. But now, he searched his memory for the details. Maybe they would help him.

"We have to find him, Mom." Edward was more worried than he thought he'd be. He wasn't even sure he liked William, but he still wanted him to be okay. He looked back at Sully's partially covered body—the second human death he had been close to. Although Sully had been there for hours, his soul hadn't gone far. They could still feel him in the home: the heartache, and the cold, stagnant feeling of grief.

How had William been able to survive that? Edward shuddered.

Flor watched her son process the moment. When he looked back up at her, she answered his question. "The mountain will guide us to him. It is time to listen for the guidance and trust that William is safe."

She gathered a few empty bottles, quickly washing and filling them with water. Although she felt William was safe and in loving hands, she also felt that time was of the essence, and the boy would be in need of water and food. She debated going home first to retrieve better supplies but trusted that her healing bag and the water would suffice. When Edward came home, Flor had called Mr. Samuels to notify him and ask that he bring help to William's house. There was no phone here, so she left a note for the others when they arrived—as she knew they would.

"Son, you have a choice to stay and wait for the others or come with me to find William. What does your heart say?"

"I want to come with you. I want to help if I can."

"I am glad for your answer. Let's begin." She led the way out the door, hanging the note on the mail clip. Once outside, she paused and closed her eyes. Edward watched and followed her lead. She noticed a slight breeze swirling to the right of where she was. She opened her eyes and confirmed the leaves playing along a very slight path. She pointed it out to Edward and waited for him to confirm he saw it too. This was the first time his lessons had an urgent edge to them.

They followed the path shown to them without questioning it, despite it being an unlikely path to choose. A hiker in the daytime would not have judged it to be a path at all.

"Should we call to him?" Edward asked with concern.

"We are still too far for him to hear our voices, but you can talk to him with your heart."

"But what if he doesn't know how to do that?" Edward had only ever practiced that with his mother.

"It doesn't matter if he knows what his heart is hearing. His heart will still hear."

Edward did just that. For the next few hours—the rest of the climb until they found him—Edward's heart talked to William's. "We're coming to help. We'll be there soon. You'll be okay."

Flor only spoke to respond to Edward or to provide direction or reminder of a lesson. She was conversing with the mountain, trees, and boulders, not to mention the animals, asking for swift guidance to find William and for his continued protection. Not from worry, but rather from expedience. The sooner they found him, the sooner they could return home and begin healing, learning, and living.

The mountain was happy to oblige. William was born of the mountain though he had no knowledge or understanding of that. Maren was of the mountain, of Star Junction. She moved away, but the mountain was a part of her and she it. William felt to climb that night because the mountain called him home to heal, to release. She, the mountain, had been waiting for this reunion since he arrived in Star Junction.

William was calm again. He started to look for a path and slipped. Then he followed one to a dead end and then a cliff. He became exasperated and afraid, but then he saw a rabbit. His mind went to watching it. Birdsong caught his attention along with a slight breeze. He didn't know why, but it all made things seem better. He watched the rabbit and followed it out of curiosity. Just on the other side of the corner bush it passed lay a small meadow. He looked all around and noticed the way the trees lined it. He headed for the trees. In the very least, he figured, he would find some shade. He also found a stream.

William was hungry walking through the meadow to the stream. He hadn't thought about food when he left the house. Didn't consider that he hadn't eaten since the day before. He kneeled to take his first sips of water from the stream and sat on a rock by its edge.

"Thanks, stream, for the water. I was really thirsty." He startled himself a little with talking, but it felt good, somehow. Like he was less alone. "I think I made a mistake coming out without supplies. I didn't know how far I'd go. But I feel kind of dumb, now."

The stream trickled past his feet along the small rocks and pebbles. Across the stream a raven landed by a bush and started pulling berries off. William didn't realize what it was doing at first but then looked closer at the bush.

"What kind of berries are those? Are they good?" The raven grabbed a couple more and bobbed up and down. William looked around for other bushes like that. He crossed the stream and examined the bush. "I don't really know what kind of berries these are. They don't look like berries I've had before."

He tried to remember anything he could about what berries were safe. He closed his eyes and asked, "Are these safe for me to eat?" He didn't know who he was asking, but he asked anyway.

He decided to try one. It tasted okay. A little sweet and tart. He waited a few minutes to see how he felt and then decided to eat more. Not that there were enough berries to satisfy his hunger, but the little sweetness tasted good and seemed to help perk him up. He would later learn that the berries were wild currants. And were, indeed, both safe and good to eat.

———

Flor and Edward came upon the enclosure that had held William for the night. Flor couldn't help but smile. She knew he had been well-protected in this space. It was very much shaped like a womb.

"What is this place?" asked Edward.

"What does it feel like?"

Edward paused and closed his eyes. He couldn't find the words for what it felt like. "I don't know how to say it. I guess, comfort."

"Hmmm, that is a good start. Keep asking within for the answer and this place itself. You will find it."

"Why are there paw prints everywhere?"

Flor smiled again. She hadn't noticed the added layer until Edward asked. "Ahh, that is an excellent observation, son. It seems it was not just the mountain that was taking care of William last night."

Edward knelt down and touched some of the paw prints. He had not paid much attention to the stories of his mother or elders in the past. Not beyond the entertainment of them. Despite some of what he had witnessed in the past, in this moment, all those stories became real. Feeling the presence of the wolves that left the prints behind, feeling the energy of this place itself, he wanted to know more and understand his mother's teachings.

"Mom?"

"Yes?"

"You have told me I would someday know I was ready, that a desire would awaken in me to know the ways. I am ready now. I would like to learn if you will teach me."

"Of course, Edward. I agree. I see today that you are ready, and you have already begun." She put her hand on Edward's head in an affectionate touch. "Come, William is not far. He was led to the stream."

"How do you know?"

"The Mountain told me." She smiled. "It is not far from here, and William will have needed water by now.

"Mom? Do you know all of the mountain...like every path and section?"

"Why would I want to know it in that way?"

"Well, I mean, you grew up here and have spent so much time with it. Wouldn't you memorize all the paths?"

"Hmm, I have introduced myself and given thanks to every part of it that has wished to be known to and by me. That does not mean some parts are not keeping private, as is their right."

"But if you hike it enough, wouldn't you have to come across all of it?"

"From a place of logic, you might think that. But our mountains here are very much alive and sentient. They are perfectly capable of making areas inaccessible if they wish. And invisible. As you will learn, some things cannot be seen by the naked eye. Some things cannot be seen at all, but they can be felt, experienced, and lived. Our egos wish to check off the lists and claim knowledge or even understanding. But our hearts simply offer gratitude and acceptance of what is. Our hearts feel without claiming anything. Our minds think and claim knowledge. This is a beginning conversation, cracking open a passageway."

William sat at the base of an aspen tree by the stream. The currants were good but not filling, and he felt tired and a little nauseated. He lost himself listening to the stream, the rustling of the leaves with every slight breeze that passed through, and the various chirps and other animal noises. The birds and squirrels had gotten used to his presence and paid little attention.

He planned to find his way back to town, but he wasn't ready to start. Everything had changed. Everything would be different, and there was just too much he didn't know. Would he really live with Flor and Edward? Would Edward be okay with that? Would they ship him off somewhere else? Back home? Oh, no...he couldn't stand that. He couldn't imagine ever leaving the mountain or the trees again.

Even without his family, they felt like home. He must have dozed from a daydream because he didn't hear the footsteps.

Flor and Edward approached quietly at first, not wanting to startle William. But Edward surprised himself by his excited call, "William!"

William woke up and looked toward the mother and son, surprised. "Oh, hi..."

"Young William, we are glad to find you here. Are you okay?"

"Yes, I think so. My father... He died. I... How did you find me?"

Edward offered, "The mountain brought us to you." He smiled at William.

Flor sat on the rock next to William and opened her bag. It was clear that he was fatigued, dehydrated, and hungry. She pulled out a small cup and poured liquid from a canteen. She added some herbs and honey and stirred them.

"Drink this, William. When you have, I have some food for you to nibble."

"I'm okay, just tired. I think." But when William tried to get up, he felt dizzy. "Maybe, you are right."

He sipped at the concoction and was visibly relieved when it tasted sweet and not weird. They sat quietly with him as he came back to himself. He looked up at Edward after finishing his drink. "I'm sorry I missed class."

Edward smiled. "It's okay. Mrs. P. postponed our presentation. You haven't gotten out of doing it yet!" he teased.

William smiled for the first time. "That's good... I wouldn't want you to mess it up."

Flor smiled at their banter. When William finished the drink and was able to eat, Flor gave him some dried meat, crackers, and fruit. "Take your time eating. We can have a real meal when we get home. This is just to give you energy for the walk."

They came down an easier path and approached William's house. Mr. Samuels had arrived and summoned the coroner and others. He knew it was only a matter of time before Flor returned with the boy. William slowed when he saw the people at his house.

"Young William, I know this is not easy. We'll go in with you to gather some of your things. Clothes and items you wish to have with you for the next few days. We will figure out the rest later. Okay?"

William just nodded and let out a breath. He had managed to forget for that little bit of time while they walked quietly and attentively. His heart raced now as fear surged through his body. Flor placed her hand high on the center of his back and breathed with him. "You are not alone, son."

CHAPTER

EIGHT

T he next morning Flor found William sitting in the courtyard when she came out to do her morning prayers. He sat before the planter with the angel trumpet tree.

"That is my favorite spot, too," she greeted him warmly.

"It's like the one at the hospital chapel. I remember it. Why do you have one, too?

"The angel trumpets are powerful trees. They carry both wisdom and grace. This one was passed down to my grandparents, a gift from the generations who walked before them. The one at the chapel was my gift to all those who may come across it, brought back from my travels."

"The birds liked that one."

"You will find them playing here as well."

"What's going to happen to me?"

"What do you mean?"

"I mean, what happens now that both my parents are gone? Will I have to go back to New York?

"Is that what you want?"

"No. I never really felt like I was meant to be there."

Flor smiled at his innocent knowing. "Your heart is wise."

"I was thinking. I've been taking care of my dad all this time. I will be okay on my own. I can still work for you, helping with the chickens, and maybe pick up some more odd jobs. I know how to cook a few things and clean for myself. I can even chop wood."

"Indeed, you have built a healthy wood pile."

William felt a wave of emotion wash over him. He looked at her and felt like she knew about all the wood that didn't need to be chopped and how much he needed to chop it.

"William, you have done a fine job looking after your father and your house. Your mother and grandmother would be proud. Even your father told me what a good job you'd done. But we must address two issues. First, that house isn't suitable. I'd already made arrangements for you and your father to move into town. A house here is marked for you when you are ready. But the second thing, the most important one, is that you are not meant to be done being a child. I don't mean a small one, not helpless or without intention. It is just that once you leave childhood, it is nearly impossible to return. Do not yet leave your innocence and your playful, open, ways. There is plenty of time for you to become an adult. For now, your job in life is to continue your childhood until it is complete and not beforehand."

She paused, and they sat in silence, waiting for the birds to wake and join them. "William, you have a place here with Edward and me. You are family as Maren was family."

"Can I think about it?" Because it was a lot to take in. A lot of change to process. A part of him wished to wrap his arms around her and never let go, but a part of him wished to run back up the mountain and disappear.

"Of course. The only decision you must make today is whether you wish to go to school. The staff would understand if you wished to rest another day. And perhaps, if you are up to it, you can help us plan an appropriate service for your father."

Edward was just entering the courtyard looking for everyone

when he heard his mother offer William to stay there. He wasn't surprised and even felt it was right, but he also felt heat rising to his face and a twinge of something he had never felt before. Jealousy.

William decided to go to school. He really didn't know what else to do. Once they had gotten to Flor's the day before, they'd eaten. Then he'd slept until morning. He hadn't slept like that since Sofia had been alive. Besides, he really wanted to do the presentation with Edward that they had worked so hard on. Flor agreed that after school they would go to his house to collect more of his things. Anything he wanted to keep but didn't have room for would be boxed up for him.

While the boys were at school, Flor met with the mayor, Mr. Bishop—who also owned the music store, Bishop's Music—Mr. Samuels, Coach Rygg, and Richard Jimenez, the postman. After discovering the state of William and Sully's home a few weeks before, she had raised the issue with the town leadership. Others could not get away for the meeting but were well informed.

"Mayor, what have you found?" Flor's eyes gleamed when she called him mayor. She'd been calling him that since childhood, even though he had only been mayor for two years.

"Unfortunately, we weren't paying attention. The properties that had been abandoned generations ago were claimed illicitly. Titles were filed, and I guess no one noticed."

"When? I mean, this didn't happen recently. Did it?" Richard asked.

"No. It was twelve or thirteen years ago. And the papers were filed in Exton and Phoenix."

Flor's heart sank as her temper rose. She didn't even ask who. "What can we do about it? How do we stop any future sales?"

The mayor smiled. "Well, it turns out that we can reclaim the land. We have filed papers to condemn the properties and place the land in the city's trust as protected property, like a park. Nobody else will end up in one of those shacks."

"Well, that is good news!" Mr. Samuels had been struck by the condition of the home when he was there to help the sheriff, coroner, and community members to collect Sully's body and cordon off the house. "I'm still struggling to believe the boy had to live in that mess."

"Thank you, Mayor Bishop. Let us make sure that we have accounted for any and all abandoned properties and assure they are not in unscrupulous hands. Together, we can be vigilant. Our old friend may not be done."

"We'll all keep our eyes out. And I will mind the mail."

"Thank you, Richard. You will be post master soon. Of this, I am certain."

The boys walked home from school together. It was the first of many school commutes the two would share. On this one, they were both on a high from the presentation. The other students were asking tons of questions, and William felt seen in a positive way for the first time since his mother died. Mrs. Peterson praised both boys for their good work and entertaining presentation.

"You did a great job, Edward. You were really funny."

"Thanks. You too. I think everyone liked it. Most people here haven't ever seen the ocean. So the shells and your stories about the salt water and sand were really cool."

When they arrived home, Flor was there to greet them. "I see your presentation went well."

"How did you know?" William asked.

"She always knows... That's just her," Edward said matter-of-factly.

After the boys put their backpacks away and had a snack, Flor asked William if he was ready to go to the house.

"Yes, I think so. Can Edward come, too?"

Flor looked at Edward to see if he wanted to. With his nod, she agreed, and the three of them drove to the shack.

"Mom, I almost never see you drive."

"True, I have little need here. But I want William to be able to carry all he wishes to bring from the house. Walking could make it all hard to carry."

Yellow tape at the door announced it was a place for caution. William instinctively took a deep breath, not knowing what he would find inside. Flor had assured him that his father was no longer there. She had asked for the area around where the body had been to be cleaned up within reason to make it easier on William to walk through. He couldn't help but look at the spot, the image of his father's body forever etched in his mind. Despite the cleanup, he still walked around the edge of where his father had been to get to his bedroom.

Edward brought in some boxes that Flor had put in the car and followed William's path. Flor closed her eyes and said another prayer within. William paused when he got into his room, as if he wasn't sure what to do or where to start. Edward watched him fidget for a moment, not really sure how to help. Then something took over.

"Why don't I help put things in boxes? I bet you want all the pictures. Right?"

William looked at him with relief. "Uhh, yeah. I do. Thank you."

That was enough to create movement. Together the boys filled the boxes with William's treasures and then moved on to pack up the family memories and heirlooms. Sofia had moved many boxes that were never unpacked. Flor agreed that all of the boxes would be stored for William until he was ready to go through them. Really, until he was ready to move into his own home one day. Flor packed William's clothes, realizing that he'd outgrown most, and they would need to be replaced.

William suddenly felt the urge to clean the dishes. He didn't understand why, but he wasn't ready to leave.

"What are you doing?" Edward's tone leaned toward impatient.

"I should wash these. I shouldn't leave the house like this. It-it isn't right."

"Son, it's okay." Flor's tone was soft and warm.

"Was I just not good enough? If I had taken better care of things. Why didn't he want to be with me? Why didn't he want to try?" He sobbed into the sink until Flor came to him and held him.

"Dear boy, let it all out. His failure is not yours. He knew your light was bright, and if he had been able, he would have loved to watch you grow brighter."

Star Junction rallied for Sully's services. Though he had been reclusive in the last year, the people who had worked with him and those who had met him at the pavilion events came to pay respect and offer condolences. Flor held the reception in her courtyard, allowing all to offer William kind words and support. And since the services for his mother had been much quieter, per Sully, many included her in their words.

By now, all knew that William was born of the mountain. And those who had known Maren included her in their words. Despite the circumstance, William had never felt more acceptance or belonging. He was amazed to discover that so many had known his grandmother. Ida, Mr. Bishop, Mr. Samuels, the postman, Richard. He found it reassuring in a way he couldn't articulate.

His grandmother had been more like his private friend, a treasured memory morphed into a dreamy legend—something he held dear but couldn't quite access. And now, all of these people knew she was real. All these people had loved her. Maybe that meant they could love him, too.

NINE

William waited in his room. The sun hadn't yet come to light the day. He listened for the sounds of Flor passing by his room and then going outside. In the few weeks since he had been there with Flor and Edward, he had noticed her patterns. Some of them, anyway. Every morning, he heard her before dawn. Every morning, she quietly went outside, often sitting with the angel trumpets. Today he was resolved to watch her and find out what she was doing. She fascinated him and reminded him of his grandmother. Today, he listened carefully to hear which door she went out of and then followed as quietly as he could to watch.

Flor stood in the direction of the imminent sunrise. She held her hands to her heart and swayed just slightly as she reached her hands forward, palms up and open as if offering a gift. If William could have seen her face, he would have seen her smile and the light in her eyes reflecting the sun he could not yet see. She raised her arms above her, and they slowly, intentionally, lowered in a graceful circle, expanding out and then returning in as she breathed. The light just beginning to glow in the east.

"Would you like to join me, young William?" she asked without turning around to see him.

He gasped with surprise and then managed a hard swallow as he walked toward her.

"How did you know I was here?"

Flor smiled. "The sun whispered it to me." She took in William's expression of shock and uncertainty and held out her hand to invite him to sit with her as she approached the bench. "Besides, I could feel you watching."

"How?"

"How does one feel anything? How do you feel the wind on your face? Or the warmth of the sun? Love or joy or sorrow?" The boy shrugged, looking even more perplexed. "You pay attention with your heart. The truth of who you are. Your breath."

They sat quietly as the sun slowly peeked over the mountain. "Do not try so hard to figure it out. It is not with your mind that you will learn it."

"But isn't that how we learn? And do anything?"

"Your mind is an excellent tool. In school, it is very important. But in life, it should always be second to your greater knowing, the wisdom of your soul."

"You sound like my grandmother."

She laughed heartily. "Indeed. And for good reason."

"Grandmother Flor..."

"Yes, William?"

"Why do you come out every morning? What are you doing?"

"I am greeting the sun. Greeting the day. Giving gratitude and love. Every day, the sun rises. Every day, the sun sets and illuminates the moon. Did you know that without the sun, the moon would have no light at all?"

"Not even when it is full?"

"Not at all. It is the sun's light that the moon reflects for us. Reminding us that even in darkness, there is light. Even in the night, we can see the shadows."

"But why do you greet it every day? I mean, it comes anyway. It's just how it works."

"Is it? I greet the sun as I pray in the morning. To let Spirit know my gratitude and joy at each new day. It is my celebration of life to start each day and my reverence to embrace rest at night."

"But what if you don't feel joy?" He hung his head with the question, allowing only his eyes to watch for her reaction. "What if you are sad or angry and don't know why?"

"Don't know why life has been as it has?"

He just nodded.

Flor put her hand on William's back between his shoulder blades, reassuring his heart. "Because no matter what life brings, it also brings us the opportunity to heal, grow, and learn. Every day is new. Every day is an opportunity to heal. There will be a time when you have grown to understand that life is not an accident, and we are creators. I don't mean that this 'you,' this boy in a body, has created the loss of your parents. Not at all. It is bigger than that. And sometimes, when we are in the middle of the swamp of emotions, trauma, heartbreak, or conflict, the best thing we can do is to greet each new day with gratitude and joy, trusting that it is the sign that there is still light, and we will know that light again."

They sat in silence as the day grew brighter, allowing his tears to fall in peace. As the sun was revealing itself from behind all obstacles, she continued, "Tears are also a beautiful offering. They are the release of the heaviness inside. The letting go of things we are not meant to carry forever."

The next day William didn't wait to hear Flor. He went outside when he awoke, only to find her there waiting.

"Good morning, William."

"Good morning... so, what do I do? How do we start?"

Flor gave him a luminescent smile. "First, you learn to breathe."

"Huh? I'm already breathing."

"Yes, but you must learn to breathe a better way. Deep into your belly, not into a constricted chest. We will call them *life breaths*. Inhale through your nose." She demonstrated, exaggerating her belly expansion to make it clear. "Exhale through your mouth."

William followed her example and started yawning after a couple of breaths.

"Am I doing it wrong?"

"No, it just takes practice. People have learned to breathe in a way that doesn't serve them well. Did Maren teach you this before?"

He thought about it. "She did... I think. But I guess I forgot. I don't remember yawning so much."

"Do not worry about the yawns. Just yawn and continue on. Whenever you think about it, take a life breath. Notice how it feels. Notice how the air feels when you inhale. Notice how your body feels. Sit with your spine straight. Notice how the air feels in your mouth when you exhale. After a few breaths, how do you feel?"

"I feel like my body is... I don't know. Buzzing, kind of."

"Excellent. Notice the earth under your feet. Supporting you."

He smiled when she said that because he felt his feet tingle and get warm.

"Keep up your life breathing. Close your eyes and imagine the sun rising over the horizon. Imagine the light coming, the warmth, and all the possibilities to live, explore, learn and play, laugh, and love. Let that bring joy to you and gratitude. Speak to the sun, to Spirit, yourself, life, God, the Universe...in your heart or aloud. Whatever you feel."

And she left him alone to do just that and went about her own salutation, including her joy and gratitude that this boy had been brought back to Star Junction.

"What do we do when we are done?"

She laughed. "We begin our day...and our chores!"

The trio enjoyed another delicious breakfast of Flor's making, which on this day included fresh skillet bread with honey, fresh eggs, fruit, and radishes from the garden. Edward ate with his usual enthusiasm but was otherwise quiet. William broke the silence.

"Your mom showed me how to greet the sun today. You should join us. She could teach you, too." He didn't realize his mistake.

"You think she hasn't already taught me? I'm her son, you know."

"Yeah, of course. Sorry. Why weren't you there?"

"You can greet the sun from anywhere. You don't have to be outside."

William looked down at his plate, not sure why Edward seemed angry.

"Okay, I just wondered. Anyway, I think it is cool. I kind of feel more excited about the day."

Flor saved them. "That is good, William. It is a beneficial heart practice. If you are done with your food, why don't you go get ready for the day?"

He nodded at her, took his plate to the sink, and excused himself.

Edward had trapped himself with a second serving. Flor sat down beside him. "Son, what do you have to express?"

"I'm sorry, Mom. He just says stupid stuff sometimes."

She sat patiently with him. "What is the answer to William's question? Why didn't you greet the sun today?"

"I just didn't want to interrupt you two," he lied.

She gazed at him with love. "Every day since you were quite young, I have felt your greeting of the sun and your sweet good nights. I have grown quite accustomed to that beautiful feeling. Today, I did not feel that same thing."

He didn't want to tell her that he watched from the window. That he felt burning inside. That he really didn't like seeing her treating William like a son. Because he, Edward, was her only son. And that burning shouted in him that William needed to back off. That Flor, his mother and only his, should make him feel like he was the one she loved the most. But he couldn't say it. Wouldn't. So he sat there in the burning, not swallowing the last bite of food and avoiding her eyes.

She stayed with him in that moment until he took a breath and finally swallowed.

"My son, my love for you is infinite. Love is infinite. It is in all things, even the honest expression of something that doesn't feel like love. I feel the burning in you and wish to remind you that you can release it. You do not need to suffer with it. You cannot be pushed out of my heart or replaced. Our hearts only expand, the muscles grow. But of course, it isn't a muscle...it is love. My love for you is so great that I noticed you were not present. I missed feeling your greeting. And I am sitting with you now, reminding you, just you and me, that my love for you is eternal and unconditional."

Edward buried his head in her shoulder and held her tightly. And she wrapped her arms around him.

Later that day Edward was sitting in the courtyard on his favorite chair. Their shepherd-lab mix, Sadie, relaxed on the cool shaded tiles next to him. It was the first few days of summer break, and he was enjoying having less of a schedule. He was staring at a block of wood, examining each side until he knew where to start. He picked up his carving tool and began.

"What are you doing?" William had been half watching, half reading his book.

"What does it look like? I'm carving."

"Looks interesting. Do you know what you are making?"

Edward looked at William with feigned dismay. "I know how to start; the rest will come."

William sat and watched, which made Edward impatient.

"You know, you can do it too." He pointed at the wood blocks and the tools. There were enough to share.

"What if I can't do it?"

"You'll learn. If you want to."

That was how it began. The friendly, mildly competitive passion for creating beauty from blocks. Grandfather Mateo had taught Edward when he was just four years old. He explained it as allowing the spirit of the wood to be expressed. It was one of the last and most vivid memories Edward had of him.

Despite his uncertainty, William picked it up quickly. By the end of summer, William and Edward had both created many beautiful pieces to share at the fire festival—a result of their desire to impress each other. Flor had never seen Edward work with such focus and passion as when William shared the same hobby.

William didn't know why he said yes so easily to staying with Flor and Edward. True, as a twelve-year-old, he didn't have a lot of options. But it wasn't that. As much as he and Edward struggled to get along at first, he was drawn to Flor. She seemed magical and wise, and she had a mystery that he longed to understand. She reminded him of his mother and more, his grandmother Maren. Maren who had grown up in this place and who Flor had known. Maren who had a sparkle in her eye and an enchanting tone in her voice that he had never heard in anyone else's voice until he heard Flor speak. So when the words she spoke included: "You can stay with us. Maren's family is my family," something in him recognized it as truth. He bit his lips and nodded before looking away to hide a tear just barely formed. And maybe, just maybe, Flor could help him feel connected to family once again.

In the first summer of William living with Flor and Edward, she established the rules quickly, not that they thought they were strict rules. In fact, many of the rules felt like adventure. One of the first rules came on the first Sunday after school let out, and it came in the form of a lesson. That morning the boys came out to find a package for each of them at the kitchen table.

"What's this?" Edward was always the first to ask and the most direct.

"Open them."

The boys complied with Flor's direction and each revealed a daypack. "It is time for you to learn how to *Walk Well* with the mountain."

"You mean hike?"

"No, son. I mean we will practice walking in the company of our natural surroundings. To *walk well* is to walk with an awareness of all that is around us: the blades of grass as they bend and sway, the leaves of the trees as they dance and flutter, the sound of air as it whispers in the wind and whistles or swooshes, the glistening of dew, the babble of a stream. Bees, grasshoppers, or butterflies. Every bit of our surroundings, our world, interacts with us. Walking well means listening, noticing, and acknowledging."

And so it began. The boys had their first lesson in *walking well*. One of their responsibilities going forward was to spend time every week in this practice. To encourage the curiosity and playful state that enhanced these walks, Flor devised homework. This was when the rule of threes began. Each week the boys would take solo foraging hikes. During the school year, these happened on the weekends only.

These hikes were a minimum of three hours of walking well combined with foraging. Each would return home with: three pieces of gratitude, three bits of learning or observations, and three gifts to share of heart or abundance, like seeds or food, treasures, or beauty. Once they'd learned to walk in gratitude and share offerings of love to the earth as they went, this practice was intended to raise their level of attention and open them to whatever presented itself to be shared with the hearts of others. If they got stuck in their thoughts, the hike would feel long and hard. If they opened themselves to listen and notice, the hike would feel joyful and brief.

"Before the fall Fire Festival and your return to school in fall, after you have become truly used to walking well, we will climb Clarity Mountain together. It will be an important journey for you both."

"What is Clarity Mountain?" William assumed it was the bigger mountain peak overlooking town. He had heard people talk about Clarity Mountain, but didn't know for sure.

"It's the mountain," Edward said with an exasperated look.

"But why is it called that?"

"Clarity Mountain is a special place, a place to learn more about ourselves and improve our relationship with our world."

"Is it the one with the eye?"

"You've seen the Eye?" Edward sounded doubtful, forgetting that William's family was from here.

William just nodded.

"You will find, Young William, and Edward, that there are many surprises here, discoveries to be made, and even pathways and portals to other worlds." Flor spoke with magic in her voice and sparkles in her eyes. "The Eye is that of our Watcher, who looks over our town and people. The Watcher is a being with so much love for Star Junction that they devoted themselves to being our guardian."

Both boys stood with wide eyes and uncertainty. They couldn't wait to get started.

The next rule or responsibility began the following Saturday when the boys came into the kitchen to find Flor sitting at the table with no breakfast ready. This confused the boys since breakfast was always ready when they came out. Edward exchanged glances with William, who shrugged.

"Hi, Mom, what's for breakfast?" He thought maybe she had forgotten or perhaps was teasing them.

"Good morning, boys. That is an excellent question." That she didn't answer.

"Um, Mom?"

"Yes, Edward?"

"Breakfast?"

"Oh, yes, what would you like to make?"

"Huh?"

She smiled at the boys as she stood from the table, put a hand on each of their shoulders, and led them to the other side of the counter.

"It is time for you both to learn."

"How to make breakfast?" William asked.

"Yes, breakfast, lunch, dinner. It is time for you to learn about food, how to clean it, prepare it, season it, to love not just the efforts on the plate but every aspect of it. Food is a gift. Delicious food, a joy. It is important to understand all that goes into preparing a meal, whether simple and for one or a feast for many. So now, you will share in the kitchen duties. You are both old enough to learn and to take responsibility for more chores."

"Are we being punished?" Edward scowled.

"No, dear, you are being loved. Cooking is one of many joys you will now get to experience. You will cook with me on the weekends. And soon, you will each be responsible for preparing two breakfasts and one dinner each week. But first, you must learn. So what are we making for breakfast today?"

"I know how to make oatmeal and scrambled eggs for breakfast," William offered. "My mom taught me and I cooked for my dad and me. It wasn't always very good, though."

"How does that sound, Edward? Scrambled eggs today?"

They all agreed and began. William and Edward collected the eggs from the coop. Flor showed them how to make skillet bread since they didn't have any sliced bread to make toast. And since it was early summer, they still had some strawberries to pick. They checked the garden to see what else looked good and decided on spinach and chives. The boys enjoyed it enough that they didn't realize it was a chore or responsibility.

By the middle of the summer, the boys had established a natural rhythm for shared responsibilities. Each was to spend at least an hour a week tending the garden. This served the purpose of not only keeping the garden weeded and happy but also ensured that they learned about the plants, herbs, and trees growing there.

Flor would regularly have them monitor, gather or harvest, plant, and till. The cooking duties and gardening worked hand in hand to teach them well about growing their own foods, understanding how to prepare them, and knowing the flavors and uses of herbs and flowers as well as the temperaments of the plants themselves. They had much to learn and know, and the best way Flor knew to teach it was to give them the responsibility of doing it.

Other chores included tending the chickens and household maintenance. William excelled at repairs of most anything that was broken, nicked, or scratched. Edward discovered he didn't mind helping William or Flor, nor did he mind doing heavy lifting. He figured it would only make him stronger. They even learned how to do their own laundry, including hanging out the sheets to dry. Other discovery hikes often followed a story or teaching session by Flor, who shared the wisdom of nature. She taught them the different areas to forage for certain wild herbs, medicinal and edible plants, currants, berries, and pinyon nuts.

The day had come. When the boys entered the kitchen after greeting the sun, they found supplies set out on the table.

"All we need are your packs," Flor announced.

They quickly ran to their rooms to collect them. They looked at the assortment of supplies: dried and fresh fruit, soft bread, dried meat, canteens, herbs, and a sandwich for each of them. Flor had filled one canteen with refreshing tea that would also help with any ailments that might occur. The boys each took their share of the supplies.

William stopped at the mixed herb bundles tied with string. "What are those herbs? What are they for?"

"Those are medicinal herbs. I will teach you more about them and where to find them, but for now, you can call them the wound healers."

"Cool."

In truth, they had more supplies than they would most likely need. The lesson was understanding what to pack. They were creating a practice of preparedness and understanding. Some of what they packed would be used for offerings rather than their own fuel. A hike up Clarity Mountain could take as little as an hour or as long as a day.

With the boys ready, Flor retrieved her special walking stick from the front entry, and they headed for the mountain. Climbing was best to do in the early morning before the heat of the day climbed the mountain with them. Much easier to descend in heat than climb.

As they walked Flor spoke. "Boys, all summer you have been practicing walking well. You have learned to listen, to pay attention, and to feel your surroundings. You now know to acknowledge the help that is all around. These skills will be very important today. It is your opportunity to put all of your lessons into practice. If you are ready, we will reach the top of Clarity Mountain, and you will discover some of what is available to you there. If you are not ready, you will keep practicing, and we will return in time to climb again."

"You mean, we might not make it up to the top?"

"That's right, Edward. If you are not ready, we will not."

"But what if one of us is ready but not the other?"

"We are climbing as one today. If one is not ready, none of us are."

"But you go to the top all the time."

"Yes."

Both boys stared at her. It had never occurred to them that they might not make it all the way up.

"Can't you just guide us?"

She smiled at them.

"Indeed. I could. But that is not why we are here. This is your climb, which means it is ours together."

William and Edward seemed deflated. They walked quietly for at least five minutes. Flor waited for all the words to sink in before she spoke again.

"Why has this bothered your mood?"

"Well, I don't know. We don't want to fail."

"Who said anything about failing?"

"You did. You said we could fail and not make it up."

"No, I said if you are not yet ready, we will not reach the top. That is not failing."

"It sounds like failing."

"Have you already forgotten the lesson of *walking well*?"

The boys shrugged.

"Why do we walk?"

"To appreciate all that is around us?" William offered.

"Are you asking?"

"Sort of..."

"What else?"

"To be present with what is around us: nature, all the animals, and life."

"Excellent. So why would this day be different? The purpose is the journey, not the top."

Edward got it. "And we should enjoy the journey... have fun even."

"Good idea, son."

The boys did just that, so much so that their climb was just under three hours. In that time Flor paid careful attention to note what they each understood and the areas that could use a bit more time and practice. They did so well that she was reassured about William's addition to the family.

When he started sensing they must be close, Edward forged ahead, his excitement not containable. William was close behind but didn't want to rush. Something told him to slow down and feel each moment beyond the excitement of reaching the top.

"We made it!" Edward's voice was loud and joyous. He was so excited about reaching what felt like the top since everything sort of flattened out. He hadn't even looked around to see what was there.

Flor and William joined him on the spot of his declaration. She enjoyed her son's enthusiasm. She also knew she had more to teach. "Have we? How do you know?"

Edward and William both looked around. "Well, there's no more up, for one thing."

"And what do you feel here?"

Edward recognized the signal to ground and go within, having let the excitement take over.

William was already there. "I feel... I don't know how to describe it. Like, expanded."

"Very good, William. And what do you notice or discover here?"

"It is peaceful. And there is a large circle over there. I can see the edges, and it looks like something is in the middle."

"And markers at the directions!" Edward had caught up.

"Very good. Let's go to the circle. Each of you take a moment and then tell me what you feel."

Edward and William exchanged looks and shrugged slightly. Edward went first. Before entering, they both walked around the circle to try to sense how or where to enter. Both were very much aware that they were being tested in a way, and both chose to enter from the east.

They closed their eyes, asked permission, and laid a small offering of herbs at the marker. Once inside the circle, they wandered a bit, but each landed in the center and then stood there, looking in each direction. They were partly trying to figure out what they were supposed to do and partly allowing the circle to guide them. Edward remembered his mom talking about the directions when he was little: east, south, west, north. Should he have started at the north? He wasn't sure. He tried to remember the lesson and was soon distracted by the thoughts.

Flor invited both boys to sit with her in the center. They took off their packs and took out the sandwiches and fruit.

"Edward, please tell me of your experience."

"I walked around the circle to see which spot I should enter from. It seemed like it made a difference, but maybe I was trying to remember something you taught me when I was little. I really felt like I should enter from the east, so I did. It was interesting to look in all the directions. I was trying to remember what you taught me about the directions. Like the east being beginnings. Like a new day. New dawn. But then I got inside my head and wasn't feeling anymore. Sorry."

"That is excellent, Edward. No need to be sorry. We are all just learning on this journey. You just shared a great deal of self-aware-ness. When you realize you are in your thoughts, you can choose differently. Well done." She smiled at Edward and took a sip of water. "William, will you please share your experience?"

"Okay. When we started to get close, I was feeling like the circle was pulling me in. I went around the outside, but all I wanted was to be in. I don't actually remember moving to the center, but as I turned to each direction I felt... I don't know, like a shaft of light or energy. I don't know what it is called. Each one felt different, and I felt different in them. I'm not sure that this makes sense at all, but I felt like each one was like a different perspective."

"Yeah, I felt that too. Sorry, I didn't mean to interrupt."

"You both have done very well. And you see, this is part of the journey that was meant for you today."

"What is the circle for?"

"Many call it the Circle of Perspective. Climbing Clarity Moun-tain is all about seeing yourself, your beliefs, and the stories you hold clearly. About dispelling the illusions we cast upon ourselves. Once here, we can bring an issue or perceived problem to the circle. By laying it in the center and facing each direction, we are gifted different perspectives of the issue, other than the one-dimensional story we tell ourselves. Each direction holds the issue in the energy of that direction. There are differing views of what the directions mean, but what is important is understanding that each can bring a different light upon any issue, any memory, any moment. The Circle of Perspective is a tool to help us look beyond wrong and right, black and white."

As they returned home, the boys' curiosity soared, each aching to know and understand more. Flor sensed this.

"Boys, are you ready to increase your understanding?"

"Yes!" they both answered.

"You are sure?"

They nodded enthusiastically.

"Please, I truly would like to understand more about what you have been teaching. I think we both would." William spoke for Edward.

"Then you will both begin attending our talking fires. Every week you will join me and the others. As I have told you before, these are not for you to talk about with those who do not attend. Everyone must come in their own timing and not before."

School started again with ease. The boys seemed to find their grooves as William began to study more and excel in classes while Edward established his role as a popular leader and athlete. For the first part of seventh grade, they spent a lot of time apart at school but together after school and on weekends. Mostly.

One Saturday morning in the late fall, Flor left the boys to themselves for a few hours as she had clients in town. At breakfast Edward had talked of wanting to play soccer with friends and maybe hike. William was going to read the latest book Ida had shared with him.

William was in the courtyard when he heard Edward on the

phone with his friend. "No, just me... Because I don't want him to... Yeah, my mom will be fine with it."

William came inside to go to his room. He couldn't help but look at Edward.

Edward caught the glance as he was hanging up the phone and suddenly felt guilty and defensive. He tried to pass it off. "How's your book?"

"It's good. Were you talking about me?"

"What do you mean?"

"Just now, on the phone. Were you talking about me. Not wanting me to join?"

"It wasn't like that. You said you wanted to read today. Besides, these are *my* friends."

"Yeah. And Flor is *your* mom."

"Yeah, she *is*. You know, I'm allowed to have friends and do things without you."

"I know." William continued to his room.

Edward left to meet his friends. He didn't want to feel guilty and didn't know why he did. He wasn't wrong. They were his friends. He shouldn't have to include William in everything just because he was there. William should make some friends of his own.

By the time Edward reached the park to play soccer, he was frustrated. His thoughts were working hard to justify his stance, to be right, fighting against a different message that he felt inside. The whisper: "If I'm so right, why do I feel so bad?" echoed within.

Edward's friends greeted him. "We're glad you didn't bring him. He's weird."

Edward broke. "He's not weird. Geez, guys, his family died, and he doesn't know anybody. And you guys treat him like a freak instead of getting to know him."

"Like you're any better. You do the same."

"Did the same. I was a jerk. But then I got to know him. You should too."

"Whatever. Are we going to play or what?"

"You guys go ahead. I have something I gotta do."

"You're ditching us?"

"Just today. It's important."

"Hey!"

"What?"

"Bring him next time."

Flor returned from errands in town to find a note from William on the kitchen table.

Dear Grandmother Flor and Edward,

Thank you for letting me stay with you. I think I am ready to go home. I didn't want to bother you. I'll be okay.

William

She wondered where Edward was and checked in his room, but he wasn't there. No note from him. She held William's note in her hand and closed her eyes.

When Flor arrived at the shack, she found William sitting, hunched over and small on the front steps. The door had been taped off and a condemned sign hung, but the door was open. William had his arms wrapped around his legs and his head buried in his knees. Flor sat next to him and remained silent.

"Where am I supposed to live? This is my home."

"Dear boy, I am sorry for you to find the house in this state. It never should have been sold to your family. We do not want anyone else to be subjected to these conditions."

"But where am I supposed to live?"

"Are you not living with Edward and me? Do you not like it there?"

"I liked it."

"Then why are you wanting to leave?"

"Because. I am my own family. You are Edward's mother. Not mine. And I can take care of myself."

"I see. But that does not work. You are still at an age where your primary job is to be a boy, a child. To go to school and to learn and absorb all of life's information that you can. One summer has not changed that. It will only be a few years before you will add adult responsibilities to your job."

"I don't understand."

"I would like for you to return to our home so you can focus on being the bright, compassionate, fun-loving boy that you are. As I have told you, when you are grown, and your wings are ready to support you, you will have a home that replaces this one. The town has already seen to it."

"I would like to. I would... but Edward doesn't want me there."

"That's not true." Edward had arrived unnoticed and stayed in the background.

William looked up, startled and confused. "Yes, it is. You said as much. I don't blame you. You didn't ask for this."

"Yes, I did. I've always asked for a brother. You can ask my mom. I just didn't think he'd be the same age and in the same class. You know? I'm just not used to it yet, you know, sharing everything."

"What are you sharing?" William asked skeptically.

"Exactly..." They both smiled. "Seriously, William. I'm sorry for what I said. I actually like having you there. I even told my friends that you were cool."

"No, you didn't."

"I did, but it doesn't matter. Just, come back. Mom needs at least one easy kid..." He winked when he said it.

Flor smiled at her son. She knew the adjustment would be challenging for him, but she loved witnessing the generosity of his spirit when he got out of his head.

William felt tall again. He contemplated everything and looked at Edward and Flor. "Okay, I'd like that. Will you let me play your drum?"

"No, duh." Edward winked again.

By the next spring, William had begun helping out enough neighbors after school that he was gifted a drum in time for the warmer weather gatherings.

CHAPTER

TEN

Eliaflore and Ikenial were great companions as they explored the wonders of Star Junction, Moon Creek, Sky River, and the mountains. The only journey they never took together was Clarity Mountain. They always made their foraging tasks for herbs and edible plants into great adventures. No one could make Eliaflore laugh like Ikenial did during their childhood.

Much to Ikenial's dismay, Eliaflore never seemed to have trouble keeping up with him, despite the age and size difference. She could climb the rocks and trees with ease. Her stamina was endless. She could even carry as big a pack as him. He tried to find things that he could beat her at but rarely did. So he acted as if he didn't care.

"Eliaflore, do you really think I was trying?" he scolded.

She would just smile and agree with him, not sure why he wouldn't be trying.

Eventually, his body outgrew hers. She would never be as tall as him, but height and strength were two different things. What he never understood was that she walked with the energy of the earth and he in spite of it.

Eliaflore sat with Ikenial at one of the school's courtyard tables during lunch. She shared her cut fruit and Grandmother Analinda's fresh-baked bread with her friend. Eliaflore had advanced quickly in school and had caught up to Ikenial by the seventh grade. This delighted her completely. Ikenial, on the other hand, had mixed feelings. But they did get to share lunch, and he was able to sneak looks at her homework without her realizing he was cheating.

"We got a letter from our friend Maren yesterday," she shared with great enthusiasm. Ikenial kept eating. "She is doing so well! Her daughter is three now!"

"Eliaflore, why do you care?"

"What do you mean, Ikenial? She is our friend."

"She was. She's gone. She left. What is the point?"

Eliaflore struggled to process what Ikenial was saying. "Oh, Ikenial, I know you don't believe that." She pushed him gently to show him she was onto him.

He rolled his eyes a bit and smiled. "You are too nice, Eliaflore. People will take advantage of you."

The school bell rang to signal that lunch time was over. They both packed up and headed back to class.

A version of this conversation repeated every time Eliaflore would receive a letter from any of those who had left. And every time, she would tell him the same thing.

ELEVEN

F lor played many roles beyond that of mother. For some she was a healer, an elder, or advisor—even a town leader. She shared wisdom and clarity. She knew most of what she did was teach. A teacher of oneself, of connection, of love. It brought her immense joy and fulfillment to witness as someone opened up another part of themselves and created pathways to Source.

Of course, children were her favorite students. She considered it a blessing that she had both Edward and William to guide and encourage every day. In the time since William had joined them, both boys had become quite proficient in their understanding of nature around them as well as their abilities to listen and pay attention. Even foraging for the edible and medicinal plants that made up Flor's arsenal of healing had become second nature to them.

Their gardening skills and intuition showed the beginning of mastery. This extended into the kitchen and the preparation of food. The boys shared in the cooking, each responsible for two breakfasts and one dinner each week. It would be fair to say that a healthy, playful level of competition had made its way into the kitchen as well.

It had been a little over two years since Sully died and William had come to live with Flor and Edward. The two boys often behaved as brothers—sometimes friends and sometimes adversaries. William excelled at school and divided his time between books and the outside, often hiking to find a good spot to read. He had become a favorite of the librarian Ida, and she encouraged his thirst with a stack of recommended books for his weekly visits. She enjoyed the freedom and challenge of finding material for him not limited to a specific genre or subject, fiction or nonfiction. From Harper Lee and Kurt Vonnegut to James Baldwin and Madeleine L'Engle, there were no limits. He rewarded her with enthusiastic reports and reviews of what he'd read.

Edward preferred the outdoors to the library and only went in when he had to. He played on the sports teams and enjoyed competition more than he would admit to his mother. In truth, he wanted to win, and he wanted to be the reason they won—the big play, save, score, whatever. He wanted to feel the satisfaction of being the hero. He tried to hide it. He knew he was supposed to be humble. He would congratulate all the others, making a show of team spirit. He felt sincere, but it seemed to him that both were true. He felt great desire to be the hero, and he knew the whole team made it work.

While the boys lived, ate, and sometimes hiked together, Flor knew they had not fully become brothers.

The annual Fire Festival marked many things in Star Junction. For the community it was a time of sharing, the beginning of harvest, the letting go of things and ways, and the celebration of community itself. It was bigger than the weekly Friday fires and held with more formality. People prepared offerings: troubles to release to the fire, or expressions of love and gratitude in the form of art, music, or food. For the kids who were so focused, it also meant that the school year would begin again soon. The freedom of summer would be replaced by school bells and structure.

Edward and William both drummed and sang hard for the festival. Flor watched with warmth and amusement as the boys both began to let go of their child-selves and claim the beginnings of their manhood. Next week, they would begin high school. In truth, it wouldn't be much different than their previous grades. But it sure felt different. The high school was a newer building that shared the same campus. It had added a gymnasium as the popularity of team sports had infiltrated Star Junction sometime around the 1940s. The field was the same one shared by the lower grades and served baseball, soccer, football, and track teams. Most of the student athletes participated in all of the sports. It was a way to exercise, or to burn off some of the extensive energy of adolescence, especially in a small town.

Both the boys had grown quite a bit in the last year, and Edward's shoulders had begun to broaden. He especially was looking forward to the challenge and competition he imagined high school sports would bring, despite the small town and most of their games being against the schools in Exton, with occasional longer drives to Fredonia, Page, and practice games with schools in Utah. Being taller felt the same as being stronger, and strength appealed to Edward.

Monday morning came quickly. William was the first to meet Flor in the garden.

"Ah, young William. Are you ready to begin your high school experience?"

William smiled at the way she asked the question. "Good morning, Grandmother Flor. Why do I get the feeling you are not asking the question it sounds like you are asking?"

"Ha!" She laughed. "Perhaps because you are wise enough to know that nothing is as simple as the label we give it."

"I'm not sure I know the whole answer. But I am glad that school begins again today. I enjoy the classes and structure. I also enjoyed all of the lessons of summer and the reading I did."

"You are a passionate student, William. Your curiosity and openness to discover will always serve you well."

Edward joined them then. "Good morning, Mom. William."

Both looked in his direction and nodded to him with smiles. Flor gave her son a loving hug.

"Good morning, son. I will ask you as well. Are you ready to begin your high school experience?"

"Of course! Why wouldn't I be?" He laughed and they joined him. Where William was reserved and thoughtful, Edward tended toward confident and boisterous.

The boys walked to the high school building for the first time as official high schoolers. Edward definitely felt different. Being in high school seemed important somehow, like he was that much closer to being an adult. He couldn't wait to be an upperclassman. In fact, the only problem with high school was that he had to start as a freshman. Star Junction didn't have the population for freshman to be swallowed up or invisible, but he wanted to stand out.

"Edward?"

"What?"

"Did you hear what I said?"

William had been talking as they always did on their morning walks to school. Only Edward's mind had drifted.

"Uhh...no." He laughed. "Sorry!" He gave William a playful push on the arm. "What were you saying?"

"I asked why you seemed so excited. I've never seen you excited about school."

"True, but this is high school. We're not little kids anymore. We get to play real sports and, I don't know, push ourselves more."

"Hmm. Well, as far as the sports go, we are still in Star Junction, so there is a limit to how many other teams we can actually play. And I don't know about you, but I've always pushed myself."

"I don't mean with studies. I mean we have so many other activities to pursue."

William laughed at his friend. "Why don't you push yourself and find our classroom?" The boys' banter had grown from tentative to brotherly, with a bit of good-natured ribbing.

Once they entered the hallway, they didn't have to look far for the classroom assignments for homeroom and first period. Mr. Samuels was there to guide the students. He served as the principal for both parts of the school. To make this easier to manage, the high school officially began the week before the lower grades. Together with some of the office staff, Mr. Samuels greeted the students and handed them their course schedules and homeroom assignments. Each student was matched with a homeroom teacher who would double as mentor and guide. Mr. Samuels smiled broadly when he saw the two boys.

"Ah, welcome, Edward, William. Good to see you both."

"Good morning, Mr. Samuels," they replied in unison. "Thank you."

Then Edward asked, "Where do we go? Did you give us a good teacher?"

Mr. Samuels enjoyed Edward's playful energy, even when it hovered the edge of demanding. "Edward..." He looked directly into the boy's eyes. "I do hope you will be pleased." Mr. Samuels retrieved the packets for each boy. "You will both be in room seven for homeroom and first period with Coach Rygg."

This time, William spoke. "Thank you, Mr. Samuels."

Room seven was down the hall and around the corner, next to the gymnasium. The large classroom had a wall of windows that provided a view of the outdoor basketball court, the playing fields, and the track. If you sat in the right spot, you could catch a glimpse of the mountain. Edward couldn't wait to play more competitively and in the big gym. The boys looked around and chose spots near the middle of the room, just slightly to the window side—a compromise of the last couple of years of sharing classes.

As they got themselves settled, and a few more students entered the room, they realized Coach was already there, standing quietly in the front of the class. The boys looked at each other a bit perplexed. *Was he here the whole time? Did he come in when we were looking at our schedules? How did we miss him?* That was the question. Coach stood about six-foot-seven with a solid build. Nothing about him was slight, yet he managed to go unnoticed for a good ten minutes before class started. Something about his stealth brought quiet to the students. Before he spoke, he held their silence and met each one's gaze with his own, a smile, and a gentle nod.

William felt himself ground and open to the mysterious start. Edward found himself amped up. Neither boy had officially met Coach Rygg before, having only seen him a handful of times at the school or the Friday night fires. He had been at some of the talking fires, but they had never spoken to him as he always seemed to disappear before the end. Even Edward couldn't remember ever meeting him.

"Welcome, class. Thank you for joining me on the first day of our journey together. Please note our rules. Despite the popular saying, these rules are not to be broken. Consider them your guidelines for success." He pointed to a sign taped to the far end of the chalkboard.

The sign read:

~ Be Respectful: always and with everyone you meet.

~ Community first: none of you are solitary beings. What affects you affects all of us.

~ Show up: this means always and in all ways. When you are here, be here.

~ Be open. This is your time to learn about life, yourselves, and each other.

~ Be curious: it is all a great mystery to be enjoyed.

~ Be on time.

~ Do your work.

~ Listen well.

~ Be courteous.

~ As of this moment, you are connected, you are community, and you are in this together.

~ Ask for help. You will find that this ability will be one of your greatest strengths in life. It is the recognition that you are not alone.

Coach watched the students thoughtfully, each day getting to know more about them than they imagined—their nuances and personalities as well as the self they presented to the world versus the one behind the masks. The second week of school he gestured to Edward and William to stay after the rest of the class left.

"Which teams will you play on?" he asked without tone. The boys looked at each other before answering.

"I want to play on all of them, Coach, if I can." Edward's answer was quick and sure.

Coach nodded and then looked to William.

"And you, son?"

"I don't know. I'm not sure I want to play any."

"I see. Which sports do you know? Maybe your father played? Or taught you?"

William felt heat wash over him, and his breath shifted. "He played a lot...baseball, basketball, and football. He would play catch with me sometimes. I wasn't very good." The memory stuck in his throat and he tried hard to swallow.

"I see. Many things change as we grow and mature. And many opportunities arise."

Edward chimed in, "Come on. It'll be fun with both of us on a team. I think you'll be great."

"I'm not really sure I want to play sports that way. You know, compete." He noticed Edward's shocked expression in response.

Coach stayed silent, reflecting upon William's answer. Edward wanted to jump in and tell William he had to play, but just before he could speak, the towering teacher sat down next to William.

"I understand, son. Sports are not everyone's cup of tea." For the first time, they saw the glint in his eyes. "But is there something to be gained from playing them? Something to be learned? Perhaps, growth to be...grown." He smiled. "Teams aren't just sports, and sports aren't just players. Can I tell you a secret?" He looked at each of the boys as they nodded. "You could take away the sports, and I would still be Coach. Life just adds the 'sport' part for fun. Ha!" With that he smacked the desk with his hand, stood up, and declared, "I expect you both to be at practice today."

Edward could barely contain his delight, and he annoyed William with it the rest of the day. But William couldn't get his mind off his father. *Why did Coach ask about him? Why would he bring him up? Surely he knew Sully was dead.* But he brought him up and so many emotions with him. By the time they had reached practice, William was resolved not only to play but to play well though the resolution swam in swirls of conflict.

It was football season. Star Junction High School being fairly small allowed the students to choose between soccer and football. Sometime in the late fifties they adopted American football as their fall season sport, electing to have soccer and track as club sports throughout most of the year.

Edward, William, and a few other freshmen showed up to the field at 2:30 p.m. and watched the team running warm up drills. Coach sent one of the players to get them practice gear and show them where to find team supplies in the locker room. By three o'clock they were back on the field. Coach smiled and sent the new players on a lap around the field—the first of many laps and many steps on their journey with Coach.

The boys returned to the house hot, tired, and sweaty. Flor smiled to herself to see their states because within all that "tired" was light and life. A new channel of energy flowed through them, and they didn't know yet what it was.

"Welcome home, boys! I see Coach recruited you."

"Mom, it was great! It's great to be able to join the teams now. I didn't think you'd mind."

"Why would I? You are in good hands."

"Did my father play sports? Coach asked William if his dad played, and it made me wonder."

"No, Ikenial did not participate much in sports...except his freshman year. But then, Coach was not a coach yet. Perhaps things would have been different if he had been."

"Yeah, he should have. William's dad played. Right, William?"

William nodded and answered quietly, "Yes. He played a lot of sports. Maybe I will take after him after all." He caught himself before the emotions rose and looked at Flor. "If it's okay, I'd like to get cleaned up before chores and dinner. And I have homework."

"Of course. You have time."

William went to his room to get cleaned up. He stopped and picked up Sully's fedora that hung on the wall and looked at the pictures that lined his mirror. Sully and Sofia. Sully after their wedding. Sully in a football uniform. Sofia holding William. Maren and William at the beach. And a picture of all four of them. William put his hand on Sully's football picture and held it there. His breaths shallow until his lungs took over and filled deeply. William just lightly nodded as he returned the hat to its hook and continued on his way.

Football season turned into basketball season, which became baseball. It turned out William had a gift for pitching, but he didn't much like the pressure. He worked hard to tune out the chants and cheers, some of the loudest from Edward. "*Strike 'em out! Use the heat! Don't let him on!*" But it was worse when a batter did get on. "*Man, you could've stuck him out. Why did you let up?*"

Coach pulled William aside before practice one day.

"Son, what's bothering you?"

"Nothing. I just—I don't know. I don't want to let people down. I don't have a killer instinct like some."

Coach laughed. "A killer instinct, huh? I see."

"I don't want to let people down."

"Any people in particular?"

William just looked over at the rest of the team and Edward.

Coach smiled. "Yep, he can be a little intense. He has a lot of spirit!" Coach put his hand on William's back and turned him to face away from the team toward Clarity Mountain. "Son, I want you to take a deep breath and tell me who you are."

William looked confused. "I'm William."

"Ah. And where are you?"

"Standing on the field."

"No, son. Where are you?"

"In Star Junction?" Coach didn't respond and waited for another answer. "On the earth?"

"No, son. You are here..." and he tapped William's head. "You are in your head. And you are not alone there."

William just looked at Coach, feeling helpless.

"You must learn to kick everybody else out of your head. All their thoughts and expectations. All their ideas of what should and shouldn't be. About you and how you pitch or don't pitch. Kick them out. They don't belong there. And then, you need to get out, too. You can't live there. Whenever the thoughts get noisy, that is your sign. Feel your feet on the earth, take deep breaths, and let go. Pitch for you. Compete only with yourself to be the best you can be. Today, that may be great. Tomorrow, it might not. It doesn't matter. Feel the earth under your feet and the air in your lungs. The rest... is play. Let it be fun."

After practice the boys walked home together. Edward was going on about how good they were in practice today and how likely they were to win the next game.

"Why do you care so much about winning?" William couldn't help himself. He wanted to understand.

"What do you mean?"

"I mean, it's all you talk about. Not doing well. Not having fun. Just winning. I just wonder why."

"Why play if you're not trying to win? Isn't that the point? To be the best. To make it worthwhile. Why don't you focus on winning more?"

"Wow. Because I think the point is having fun. Doing our best, which is not the same as being the best. There is always going to be someone better."

"That just makes you work harder."

"But what if you work harder and still don't win? Wasn't it still worth playing?"

They walked in silence until they were almost home.

"But what about your dad? I thought you decided to play to make him proud."

"Haven't I already done that? I've proven that I'm good. I can play all of the sports that he did decently well. I've shown that. If he's able to see me, I think he's proud." He took a sudden deep breath and exhaled sharply. "Yeah, at least, he should be. I'm not the wimp he was afraid I was."

"Maybe you're right, but I still want to make my dad proud...and maybe make him regret not being here." Tears edged Edward's eyes as he spoke, and William matched them, not sure what to say.

"I'm sorry...I didn't realize. He'd be an idiot not to be proud of you."

William put his hand on Edward's shoulder, and Edward did the same. They didn't remove their hands until they walked through the front patio door.

TWELVE

Twenty-Seven Years Ago

I t was Friday afternoon and Eliaflore was excited to help with the Fire Festival setup. In just a few more weeks, she would be starting her senior year of high school. She was carrying loads of supplies between the chapel hall and the Star Pavilion when she saw Ikenial crossing the street.

"Ikenial!" When he didn't respond she yelled louder and waved. "Ikenial! Hey..."

He stopped and hesitated before turning to face her.

"I heard you the first time." His tone was curt.

Eliaflore stepped back, not prepared for his unfriendliness. "Then why didn't you respond?"

"I am not at your beck and call just because we have been friends."

"Don't you mean that we are friends?"

"Whatever. Look, I've told you to call me Ike. I'm not Ikenial. I'm Ike."

"Okay, if that is what you want. I didn't realize you were serious before. Ike, will you help me carry these chairs to the pavilion?"

He looked at her and shook his head. "Look, no. I've got to go. I'm not going to the festival tonight."

"But it's the Fire Festival."

"I know what it is. I'm not going. I have other things to do." He paused and looked at her with impatience. "It's just a show, you know. They're just using you and telling a damn story. You should wake up. We could have some fun if you would."

She stood, frozen. No words came.

He shook his head again. "See ya around." He walked away.

Eliaflore walked to the pavilion, dropped the chairs, and wiped her tears. *Why am I shaking?* she wondered. She had never missed a Fire Festival, or one of the weekly fires and music. Sixteen years of fire dancing, of feeling the power of the dance, of listening to what came. *No. He is wrong.* The voice she thought it with was angry and hurt.

Grandmother Analinda found her sitting in the Star Pavilion, staring.

"My child, what is occupying your mind?"

Eliaflore was startled back to the moment. "Oh, Grandmother... Ikenial said some terrible things. He denies his name. And he said the Fire Festival and all of it is just a lie. Stories, he said. Trying to make me feel foolish for participating. How could he say such things? We have grown up together, seen the same things. Had the same teachings. I do not understand."

"I see. Ikenial does not see through your eyes or experience. We have seen for some time now that he is choosing a different path. It is his choice, Eliaflore. You know that everyone must make their choices."

"But isn't he a path keeper too?"

"Not all who are born of it will make the choices in the right vibration. Ikenial is drawn to shiny objects, like a crow. We have seen it since he was a child and tried to guide him well. But we cannot choose for him."

"But, Grandmother, what does that mean? That you have given up on him?"

"No, child. We love him regardless. He is a child of Star Junction and of this world, and he is loved. However, we suspect he will follow a worldly path rather than our star path."

"But what does that mean for me if I am his friend?"

"His path is not yours. You have shown that. Be his friend, but know there may be a time when you will have to let him go."

Eliaflore didn't want to respond, so she stayed silent as her thoughts shouted inside her head. *No! I will not let him go. I will not give up on him. I'm tired of people leaving.* Even if she knew her grandmother was right, the thought of having to let another friend go felt too hard.

"I know it is hard for you, Eliaflore. Some day you will have to discern between your worldly attachments and the truth of your path. It is possible to love without attachment."

"Oh, Grandmother, please forgive me. I don't want to lose any more friends."

Analinda hugged her granddaughter until Eliaflore let out the breath she had been holding. "Sweet child, it is one of the harder lessons. Hold the truth that your friends are not lost to you. You only need look for them in a different way. Dance with the fire tonight and talk to the stars. This is where you will feel your friends. Those who choose this path will be dancing with you."

Eliaflore danced with intensity that night, and the fire met her at every gesture, twirl, and spin. And she felt her friends dancing with her: Maren, Violetta, Rose, Ida, Zekiel, Sayari. Her heart filled knowing it was so. It held space for Ikenial but was not empty.

Just a few weeks later Ikenial, Ike, stopped going to school. Eliaflore had caught him copying her work. He shrugged it off and laughed, teasing her not to be so serious. Then she saw him steal from another student's desk. Or she thought she did, but she didn't want to believe it.

Later she was walking to Moon Creek, and he caught up to her.

"Eliaflore, Elie, wait!"

She turned toward him until he reached her and then continued to where she was headed. "Elie... I'm sorry. You shouldn't have had to see that."

"What do you mean?"

"I mean, I wish you hadn't. I shouldn't have said what I did either."

"Why did you? Why did you do any of it?"

"Look, it doesn't matter. I came to tell you I'm leaving. I just can't be here anymore."

"What! What are you talking about? This is your home."

"Nah, it's just the place I've been stuck my whole life. There's nothing for me here. I want to go see the world, drive a car, have nice things."

"Nothing? What about your friends?"

"I don't care. Except for you. You're the only one... but you hover. And still believe in all this star path crap. I don't know. I could be with you, maybe. You know? When you are ready to leave this place, and they're not all watching."

"What about finishing school? You're so close."

"Don't need it. Why would I waste more time? I've got a line on a job in Phoenix and a place to live. I've always wanted to go to the city to live a big life. I'll be making good money."

"Ikenial..."

"Ike," he said coldly.

"I'm sorry. Ike. I don't know what to say."

"Say you'll join me when you graduate. Come join me."

"Why don't you stay here until I graduate. And maybe we can go together."

"No, Elie...I can't stay. I burned the bridge."

They continued walking in silence until they reached the

widened pool that gave Moon Creek its name. Eliaflore tried to hold it all in. She held her words tightly, knowing they could cause the emotions to flood out, and then she would forever be a part of Moon Creek. She didn't dare look at him. Or shift her gaze. Or swallow.

Ike put his hands on her shoulders and then touched her face. "I hope you'll be as excited to get my letters as you have been for all the others. I've gotta go before it's too late." He leaned in and kissed her cheek and then her lips before leaving her there.

Eliaflore worked hard to graduate early. She didn't want to wait to join Ike. She also worked hard to ignore the part of her that didn't want to join him at all. Her grandparents watched her and added more lessons for her growth. They suspected she would go to find him, and they wanted her to be better prepared.

"Eliaflore, child, it is time for you to climb again. Clarity Mountain calls to you."

"I have climbed so many times. Why must I do it again?"

"It is not a must. It is a call. We know you desire to find Ikenial. He has written you many letters and told you stories filled with possibilities. You well know that the mountain path is never the same. If you are to leave, it is best to do so with clarity of vision. This is why the mountain calls."

"Then I will climb before I go, but I will go."

Eliaflore left before dawn, half expecting to greet the sun from the top of Clarity Mountain. Instead, she found herself in the *place of remembering* in view of the ever-watchful guardian as the sun began to light the day. She noticed how brightly the Eye was illuminated and released her plan.

Okay, I will talk with the guardian first. By the time she reached the Eye, another hour had passed. Her frustration grew with the loss of time. She could be on her way to Phoenix. She sat there waiting for the Watcher to speak and tell her what she was called here for.

But no words were spoken. They sat in silence together until she gave up.

She lay back and accepted she would not travel today. She would not hold a plan at all. She also surrendered the expectation of an explanation—the demand that the Watcher or the Mountain should explain themselves or justify their call to her.

Finally, she closed her eyes, relaxed her body, and spoke. "I'm sorry. Please forgive me. I came to you unwilling to hear, let alone listen."

"And why is that, dear one?"

"Because I didn't want you to tell me I shouldn't go. That I was making a mistake."

"Oh. Why would I tell you that? What is wrong with making mistakes?"

"Then why don't people want me to go?"

"Perhaps people only hope for you to go with your eyes open, your awareness on."

"Or they are hoping I will come to my senses. See what they want me to so I won't go."

"Oh, are you keeping yourself blind to something?"

"Not blind, exactly. I know what they are worried about."

"Looking directly at something allows you to make purposeful and informed choices. They are yours to make. It is your path to walk. You can walk it with purpose and clarity, or you can walk it with blinders."

"I love him. I know he... he is lost. But shouldn't we always see the good in people?"

"Wouldn't seeing the whole person be more helpful?"

Eliaflore opened her eyes but didn't respond. Her mind was trying hard to find the argument. Her desire to go to Ikenial, to be with him, overwhelmed her. Maybe if they were together, she could help him change.

"Child, it was not Ikenial you were called here for. It is yourself that you are meant to see. If you truly know yourself, all of the choices you make are truly yours."

The Watcher stopped speaking, and Eliaflore was left to continue as she chose. She chose to continue her climb and leave nothing of herself unseen. At the top of Clarity Mountain, she sat in the Circle of Perspective and stayed until the next morning. Her gift was clear visions of her path with and without Ikenial. She saw him as a whole and accepted his flaws. Most importantly, she saw herself, the openness where her boundaries should be, and how her love was overtaken by a desire that things be different than they were.

When she was able to separate how she wanted things to be and how they were, she also released her attachment. That night in her dream she accepted a gift: a layer of white light that enrobed her being as a boundary of love that deception could not penetrate. She accepted that all things are possible in love. It was possible that Ikenial could change course and carry light once more. But she also let go of the need for it to be so.

Eliaflore was no longer in a hurry to leave. She spent a few more days with her beloved grandparents and friends. The night before she left, she sat with Mateo and Analinda at their fire. They were once again enjoying Analinda's special cocoa, made with cacao, spices, and a rare indulgence of roasted marshmallows.

"Granddaughter, it is good to see you in your joy again."

Eliaflore smiled at her beloved guardians. "Thank you, Grandfather. Thank you both for holding the light."

"This is the role of a light keeper." Analinda said with a twinkle in her eye.

"Grandmother, thank you for the delicious treat."

Analinda just nodded.

"Eliaflore, your path is before you. When you are ready, and if you choose, your master journey is open to you. Let us know from wherever you are, and we will arrange the passage. If you choose it, you will have experiences beyond your dreams. You will meet others of the star path, healers, seers, wisdom keepers. They will have much to teach you."

"And I will have much to learn when I am ready."

The next day, she said goodbye to her friends Richard, Rygg, Ida, and others. She got a ride to the bus station in Exton and was on the bus to Phoenix by 9:00 a.m. It was her first time going anywhere further than Exton. The scenery fascinated her: mountains, desert, mesas, buttes, and ruins. She wasn't sure quite where they were when trees were replaced by cacti, specifically, saguaros.

She would have to study the map to see the areas they passed through. Some of them held magic that she wanted to explore. The bus arrived to her stop in Phoenix a little before 5:00 p.m. She gathered her luggage, one larger bag that had been Mateo's, and her pack that certainly wasn't ladylike but was her favorite way to carry her necessities. When Ikenial hadn't arrived by 5:15, she determined that he must have been delayed or wouldn't be able to make it. She asked the woman in the information booth for directions to the address he had given her.

Eliaflore walked two-thirds of the way there, about a mile, before a car slammed on its brakes just after passing her. The driver quickly pulled the car to the side and backed up, narrowly missing other traffic. "Elie! Elie! Get in."

Startled, she looked inside the car to find Ikenial. "Elie, I'm sorry I'm late. I got caught up in something. Get in, and I'll tell you all about it."

He swept her away to dinner followed by a walk in the park and tried to interest her in a nightcap despite being underage. Finally he took her home to his studio apartment. It had a small refrigerator, a beat-up couch, and a bed that folded up into the wall.

"Don't worry, Elie. You can have the bed. I will sleep on the couch. I'm so glad you are here." He noticed she hadn't said much. "What's wrong?"

"Nothing is wrong. This isn't quite what I pictured from your descriptions."

"Yeah, I had a setback. But it's just temporary. I promise. Tomorrow, I will show you the university, if that's what you still want, and more of town. I'll introduce you to my friends."

Ikenial was true to his word. He showed her the university campus. They walked the campus. He told her how wonderful it was that she was there now. Now things could really get better. Really begin. He was sure his luck would change now that she was there with him. She learned that he'd had many different jobs since moving there under a year ago, all of them ending for some unfortunate reason or another.

He knew where campus was because he had worked there for two of the jobs, not because he had somehow become a student despite not graduating high school. Although they had spent the first night at his place with him spinning tales for her amazement, he explained that most nights he would be working at a club, helping a friend.

After a few days, Eliaflore decided to venture out on her own. Ike had claimed to have to work that day. She went back to the university to talk to an advisor to find out what her options were if she wanted to attend. She visited a couple of shops and a bakery, inquiring about possible employment.

What she had seen so far was that Ikenial was struggling. She could see his lies now, see the energy around his words. Before making a decision, she wanted to explore the options for her there, with or without Ikenial. The university said if her grades were satisfactory, she might be able to apply for the spring term.

The co-owner of Betty's Bakery invited her to sit for tea and whatever treat she would like. Eliaflore felt at home with the delicious aromas of fresh baked treats and generous sprinkling of stars in the décor. They talked about baking, the available job, and Phoenix. Long into the lively conversation, the woman took Eliaflore's hand and looked her in the eyes. "Our paths take interesting turns. Don't they?"

Eliaflore knew then that the woman held the light. And whatever decision she made would determine the next turn. "Thank you, ma'am, for your time and conversation."

Eliaflore returned to Ike's around 3:00 p.m., expecting him to be at work. She had returned with treats from the bakery and the determination to cook them dinner on his hotplate. When she opened the door, she found Ikenial and his friend Maria naked and engaged on the bed.

"Oh crap! Elie, what are you doing here so..." He stopped, realizing there were no more words to that question that made sense. Ike scrambled to disengage and wrap a sheet around him, leaving Maria to fend for herself. "Elie..."

Eliaflore paused and took it all in, navigating the different emotions that arose and landed firmly on acceptance and relief. "I see you are hard at work. Sorry to have interrupted."

Maria looked at Eliaflore and then Ike. She smacked him when she realized he wasn't worried about her in the least. She used the blanket to cover up, grabbed her clothes, and disappeared into the bathroom. Eliaflore and Ikenial waited in silence until Maria returned fully clothed, grabbed her bag, and smacked Ike again. "Don't call me!" She stormed out.

"Elie, I know you're not ready for this part of our relationship. I didn't want to pressure you. But I'm a man. I have needs."

Eliaflore looked amused. "Oh, I see. A man of nineteen with needs. Ikenial..." She paused with a long look at him. "Ike, I made a decision today. One that you have graciously validated. I came home with a plan to cook us a goodbye dinner. But I think that is no longer necessary."

"Elie, don't go. You just haven't been here long enough. We'll figure it out."

"No, we won't. I love you, Ikenial. I don't know how to love Ike. We are too young and not ready for what you say you want. This just proves that. Be Ike. Figure it out. Who knows? Maybe we will have another chance in the future."

She calmly gathered the few items that weren't already in her bag. She really hadn't had room to unpack. She kissed him on the forehead and went, leaving the food for dinner but keeping the bakery treats.

Eliaflore found a payphone near the park and called her grandparents. Delighted, they told her about a bakery near the university. Betty's Bakery. "That's where I went today." Eliaflore opened her bag of treats and found a brochure for an old chapel. She returned to the bakery and Betty's husband Matthew drove her to the chapel. From there, her journey would begin.

THIRTEEN

S tar Junction had a unique climate. Tucked somewhere near the border of northern Arizona and southern Utah, in a mountainous uplift not too far from the Grand Canyon's North Rim, it enjoyed the benefits and challenges of high altitude and interesting thermal patterns. The lower areas show off juniper and pinyon pines. Aspen groves could be found in the mountains with ponderosa pines at even higher elevations. The appearance of other species defied logic, and if those who studied such things were to visit, they might find themselves baffled by what they thought they knew, perhaps not fully understanding the essence of the plants and trees themselves.

The summers were cooler than the lower regions, but something about altitude made one feel closer to the sun. For the residents of Star Junction, William and Edward specifically, the heat of summer meant finding ways to stay cool—typically including excursions to the river and creeks. It also meant early morning or nighttime hikes. One of their new practices was to leave around dusk, find a place to camp for the night, and return home in the early morning sun to share the story of the experience. Flor was an exceptional audience for those stories. The boys alternated solo and shared experiences.

The heat of summer was also the season for monsoons full of thunderstorms that provided much appreciated water and put on quite a show. The boys knew when to seek cover. Lightning was no force to be careless with. On one memorable outing, they managed to duck into a cave just before lightning struck a tree not fifty feet away. They didn't want to repeat that lesson—and never took the weather lightly again. Before they knew it, summer was nearly over and their school year was about to begin.

As returning players, the boys started football practice a few weeks before school began. On their way home from practice one day, they saw two new students as they were exiting the school doors.

Edward broke the ice. "Hey, are you new here?"

The older of the two, a beautiful girl whose long hair shimmered in the sun, looked up, somewhat startled. She and the boy walked closer. "Yes, we just moved here."

"Okay."

William gave Edward a questioning look and a playful smack on the arm. Then he turned to the beautiful girl, "Welcome. I'm William. This is Edward."

"Thank you. I'm Grace. This is my brother Ray."

"What year are you?"

"I'm a freshman and Ray is in seventh grade. We just met with Mr. Samuels to get registered."

"Without your parents?" Edward asked.

Again, William smacked him lightly.

"My dad spoke with him on the phone and sent all the paper-work with me."

"Well, if you need anything, let us know. We'd be happy to help or show you around town."

"Thank you."

Ray never spoke. He just nodded and watched. Grace was polite but noticeably contained.

"See you around," Edward said as he and William started to walk away. Suddenly William turned back.

"Have you been to the Friday night fires yet?"

"No, what is that?"

"You should come. It's at the Star Pavilion in the park." He pointed in the direction. "In the center of town. Every Friday. Everyone is welcome. It's fun."

"And there's food!" Edward was always enthusiastic about food.

Edward kept glancing at William on the walk home and smiling.

"What was with you back there?"

"What are you talking about?"

"You should come...it's fun," he said in a mocking voice and laughed playfully.

"What? I was being friendly and welcoming. Something I didn't get when I moved here."

"Yeah okay. You're right. But we've made up for it since." He couldn't help himself. "I think you like her."

William rolled his eyes and laughed. "You are relentless."

The boys entered the house and breathed in the intoxicating aromas. Despite their efforts, they couldn't compete with Flor's cooking.

"Mmmm, Mom.... That smells delicious!" He beamed at Flor, who was rolling out flatbreads. "Can we skip chores and just start eating?"

"Welcome home, boys. I appreciate your enthusiasm, son."

"We met a new girl and her brother today. They just moved to town."

"William likes her!"

"I was being friendly. You should try it. I invited her to Friday's fire."

"Excellent. Mr. Samuels let me know as well. I will make sure to greet them tomorrow and reinforce your invitation."

They enjoyed a dinner of river trout, grilled vegetables from the garden, and hot flatbreads with herbs and garlic.

"Mom, nobody's food tastes like yours."

"The secret is love. Plant with love. Harvest with love. Prepare with love. Love of the ingredients. Love of those who will consume it."

Something struck William just then. "That reminds me of something my grandmother would say. She was also a great cook...but the flavors were different."

"Ah, yes. Maren knew well about love. But not all flavors are available everywhere. I learned of many of the spices I use from my travels."

"I didn't know you traveled. What do you mean? Where did you go? When?" Edward asked.

"I traveled before you were a gleam in my eye. Before returning to Star Junction to finish my training and accept my staff."

The boys just stared at her.

"When I was young, a little older than you both. I left after graduating high school to be with someone I loved. But when that proved to be ill-fated, I began a journey to receive teachings from other star junctions. Grandfather Mateo and Grandmother Analinda had arranged for my master journey. I traveled to many other lands: Mexico, Hawaii, Peru, the Andes, the Amazon rain forest, and even Europe.

"I learned about medicinal plants and practices in each place. I learned of techniques as I bonded with the natural elements, and I learned about their foods, spices, and specialties. I shared with them all I knew, and they shared with me all I could fill myself up with. And seeds. I brought the seeds home, and they continue to thrive in our garden.

"When I arrived home, Mateo and Analinda determined that I was ready for my journey of many days. One day, you may also find yourselves on a journey of many days, should you choose to continue the star path."

The boys listened intently, but Edward's energy dropped. He wanted to know all she had to teach, but his attention stopped at "someone I loved" and "ill-fated."

"I sent some of the seeds to Maren, and she shared some of the seeds of her travels and recipes."

"Are you talking about my father?"

Flor paused and looked at him with love.

"When you said 'someone I loved' and 'ill-fated,' were you talking about my father?"

"Yes, Edward. I was speaking of Ikenial. I missed him terribly when he left Star Junction. He wrote me often to convince me to join him. Despite Grandfather Mateo's and Grandmother Analinda's concerns, as well as my own doubts, I went to be with him. I was going to go to college there...where I thought he was doing the same."

"But?"

"We were young and were not ready for that kind of being together. He made that clear to me, and we parted. Mateo had made arrangements with other elders for my transportation on the first leg of the journey. I accepted. It was my path. I knew it to be true."

"So, you didn't get married then?"

"No. Not then. Not until after I returned from my travels and training and had accepted my role and staff."

She watched her son closely, feeling his energy and watching his thoughts spin. Edward didn't ask more questions. He wasn't sure he wanted to hear the answers.

On the hotter days, summer football practice took place in the morning before the heat of the long day set in. After school, and since it was Friday, Edward went to his job at the gas station that

Coach owned. He desperately wanted to earn enough money to buy his own car as soon as possible. The idea of a car felt like freedom though from what, he didn't know.

In anticipation of being able to drive, both boys had started restoring William's old Nomad that Sully had driven the family to Star Junction in. It had been sitting for nearly six years. The agreement with Flor for both of the boys was that the responsibilities of school came first, which included their practice of her teachings. She approved of all of their chosen work opportunities: the gas station with Coach, Bishop's music store, the market, and learning carpentry and building.

It was William's turn to stop at the market for Flor's order. He was looking forward to getting home, prepping a snack, and reading before heading to the Friday fire. In fact, his mind was already on the book that Ida had chosen for him last week, *The Hero with a Thousand Faces* by Joseph Campbell. William was captivated and distracted by it. As he came to the market door, he almost passed it completely. He turned so abruptly that he nearly knocked over the person coming out. Grace.

"Oh, excuse me! Sorry about that."

Both their hands were on her grocery bag.

"It's alright. No harm done." She smiled when she said it, and William couldn't take his eyes off of her. "Are you okay?"

He shook his head to clear the spell. "Yes, sorry. I guess I was just distracted."

"By shopping?"

"No, um...a book I'm reading." They both stood there in a moment of awkward silence. "I should let you get back to it. Nice to see you, though."

"Nice to see you, too, William."

He smiled as she started to move, but he was still holding the grocery bag.

"Oh, sorry." He let go, and she started to the sidewalk. He called after her, "Grace."

"Yes?"

"Are you going tonight—to the Friday night fire?"

"I don't know. What time?"

"People start around five, but it can go 'til ten or so. It's a good way for you to meet people. Lots of families. And food... lots of food to share."

"Okay, I'll see if we can."

"Great."

Flor and William set up the food tables—one for pantry items for all to share and two for prepared foods and desserts. William loved this part. He knew what it felt like to be without food and staples. Since William's first Friday fire experience hiding with Sir, the town had made lots of accommodations to make sure those in need could receive with grace. They even had many foods in containers that people could take and return clean to the community center when they were done with them. And the pantry at the community center was open every day.

"All of the food looks and smells amazing tonight!" He beamed. Flor watched him, somewhat entertained by his enthusiasm. She noticed that he looked up from what he was doing every few minutes and scanned the park.

"I'm glad you approve."

"Well, of course, it's always good. Maybe I'm just extra hungry." He smiled when he said it and again scanned the park.

"Who are you expecting?"

"I guess I am being too obvious. Huh? I don't know why. I'm hoping Grace will come. I ran into her at the market today and reminded her."

Flor's smile radiated joy. "It is nice to see you this way. If she does not make it tonight, there will be many more opportunities. She will come."

Edward made his way toward them.

"Hey, William! You ready?"

"Oh, yep. Sure."

He shot one more glance around the park before heading over to the group of musicians. William had become an excellent drummer and flute player in the last few years. Recently, both boys had taken up guitar, but that was for other moments. Friday nights were for drumming, dancing, and celebrating another week. Something about drums helped everyone let go, release the stress and craziness of the week, and have some fun.

Edward noticed William's distractedness as they got their drums set up.

"What is with you?"

"What do you mean?"

"I mean you're everywhere but here."

"Sorry. Just thought..." He stopped talking because he saw Grace down by the food tables with Ray.

Edward watched his friend for a moment, entertained that he just stopped in mid-sentence. Then he whacked William's arm to wake him up.

"Man, something is wrong with you!" he said with a smile.

William shrugged and smiled.

"I just want her know she has friends here."

"Yeah, sure. Let's get started."

Flor showed Grace and Ray the bounty of foods and containers they were welcome to use. "We are a community that takes care of each other."

Ray was the most excited. "Wow, we can have any of this?"

"You can have whatever you want." She smiled at the boy and patted his shoulder.

Grace looked less excited, even pensive.

"What is your concern, Grace?"

"This is the kind of thing our mother would have helped with. But we never would have taken anything without contributing. I wish I could help, but I really only know how to make a couple of meals. Even Ray is getting tired of them," she said as she looked at her little brother.

"That's not true! I like everything you make."

Flor beamed at them. She saw their deep love for one another.

"Ah, I see. It sounds like your mother was a good woman and a good teacher. She just didn't have long enough with you."

Grace nodded politely.

"Please come to the house tomorrow. You will cook with me, and it will give us all time to get to know each other."

Grace smiled and quickly looked down to hide her blush.

Ray chimed in, "Can I come?"

"Of course."

William managed to keep his focus once he started drumming. But that was as long as it lasted. When they finished and approached the food tables, Grace was all he could see.

"Ahh, the boys are back."

FOURTEEN

E liaflore drove all night to get there. After over two years working with teachers around the world, training in the ways of healing, plant medicine from cacao to ayahuasca, energy, and the stars, the call finally brought her home. The closer she got, the more she lit up. She felt her grandparents the most and felt there was a reason for the call. When she left, she never imagined having a car or needing one. But on her journey, it was gifted to her in gratitude for her work. The generous gift made her trip home possible in a day's time. It was strange to drive this road, but she was glad she could. When she pulled into town, the sun was just beginning to break on the horizon. She let out a deep breath as tears clung to the corners of her eyes.

"Hello, home... I have missed you so."

The trees rustled as she drove by.

She pulled as close to the compound as she could, the road still rustic dirt. As Eliaflore entered through the front patio, the herbs and flowers welcomed her with their vibrant scents. She was not surprised to see the light on inside. They were always up with the sun to greet each day. She closed her eyes and said thank you for the greeting before continuing inside. Then she headed to the back courtyard to find them. Mateo was there by the angel trumpets, but Analinda was not in sight.

"Grandfather?"

"Hello, granddaughter. Welcome home." He rose and came to her.

She couldn't help but hug him tightly.

"It is so good to be home. Where is Grandmother?"

He cupped her face in his hands.

"She is inside. Come. You can help."

Eliaflore just nodded. She suddenly felt uneasy. Mateo put his arm around her shoulder and walked with her to his and Analinda's bedroom. Analinda was there in a wheelchair, greeting the sun through the window.

"Grandmother!" Eliaflore rushed to Analinda, kneeling to embrace her. "I'm so happy to see you. Are you okay?"

"Eliaflore, child, you are good medicine. I too am happy."

Eliaflore got to work in the kitchen. She had learned many things on her journey, including delicious foods she wanted so to share with her grandparents. First, she helped with a deep cleaning. It wasn't that the kitchen was dirty, but it felt a good way to show gratitude and appreciation.

Then she retrieved some of the ingredients she had brought with her. Spices that she had never heard of or had before her travels. Grains that were new to her. Oils. Dried fruits, herbs, and delicacies that made her beam. For many of the items, she was able to obtain seeds and instructions for growth. Others she hoped would be sent from afar. She'd traded for some of the seeds, herbs, currants, and pinyon nuts that were abundant here.

First, she made a whole grain bread dough and let it proof as she made a Peruvian sopa de quinoa con pollo. As she watched her grandmother in her morning prayers, she thought of this soup that she had found so nourishing during her travels. Other than the quinoa and spices, her grandparents already had the ingredients. Cooking had always been one of her best conductors of love.

The warm crusty bread was perfect for sopping up the flavorful broth. Mateo and Analinda were intrigued by the subtle spice and the quinoa itself.

"Eliaflore, you have brought back treasures with you," Mateo said with a smile. "Thank you for sharing this with us. We have missed your cooking." He winked at his granddaughter playfully.

"Your grandfather is right. What is the little grain?"

"That is quinoa from Peru. I fell in love with this soup there, and so many flavors of the world. I learned much about the healing properties of the ingredients, spices and herbs. I hope you will enjoy them as I do."

The grandparents looked at her with love and waited. Eliaflore noticed the shift and stopped the flow of words.

"I feel I have missed much here." She looked at Analinda when she said it and then shifted her gaze. "Was I gone too long?"

"No dear, all is in perfect timing." Analinda took Eliaflore's hand in hers. "You cannot miss what was not meant for you. And you are here just in time for what is."

Eliaflore noticed the uneasy feeling return. She swallowed the lump that had formed in her throat and asked, "What is?"

Mateo patted Analinda's hand then held it gently. "Granddaughter, we are not getting younger. It is time to begin the transition—for you to step into the role you have always been aimed for—and for us to help you. You still have more to learn. We must teach you while we are still able."

Eliaflore had never wanted to think about her grandparents getting older. They certainly didn't age as she had seen others. The comparison had tricked her into believing what she wished to be true —that she would have them forever. The ill feeling occupied her, and she felt tears come as she searched for the way to get the words out.

"Grandmother, Grandfather, I do not know if I am indeed ready, but I trust in your guidance. If I am not now, you will help me to be in perfect timing. Truthfully, I feel as if I am far too young to be an elder, but I know it is not about age."

"You see, granddaughter, you are far more ready than you imagine." Analinda radiated her love. "The change will not be immediate, but the training must begin. As you know, you will have challenges and challengers. Your strength is always in knowing your truth."

That night Eliaflore sat with her grandparents by the fire pit in the courtyard. Of all the beautiful places she had traveled in the last few years, she didn't think any could top this. Of course, this was the magic feeling she knew so well. The moon and stars put on a good show, and she smiled to think it was for her.

"Our stars have missed you."

Eliaflore smiled at her grandmother. "I think they know I have missed them. And I have missed home. But I am truly grateful for all I experienced, witnessed, and learned."

"For all of it?" Analinda prodded.

"Yes." Eliaflore had shared some of the story of Ikenial in her letters. "Even for what happened with Ikenial. He showed himself to me. That was a gift. It allowed me to decide. To know clearly that my path was not in Phoenix with him no matter how much I wished it to be different."

"That was a gift, truly," Mateo agreed. "You have grown in your wisdom. Do you think he will return?"

Eliaflore was taken aback by the question. "I cannot say. This was his home, though he didn't feel connected to it as we do."

"And if he did?"

"I'm not certain what you are asking. We have not been in contact since the day I left him and began my journey. I do have love for Ikenial. That will not go away. But I also have clarity. And perspective. I know my path and choose to walk it with focus and devotion."

"Ah, that is good." Mateo exchanged a brief look with his beloved and changed the subject. "Have you been working with portals?"

"What do you mean?"

"In your travels, at the trainings, did you learn about portals?"

"We talked about different kinds of portals and vortexes."

"Excellent. You have known of many vortexes here."

"Yes, there are many on the mountain. And in this yard." She smiled and looked to the angel trumpets.

"It is time for you to work with the vortexes and discover and explore the portals. Recognizing them, understanding them, and mastering them is essential for you on this path. Tonight, you will begin. Sit with the vortexes in our yard. See what they will share with you."

With that Mateo stood, kissed his granddaughter on the forehead, and wheeled Analinda closer to say goodnight before leaving Eliaflore to be with the stars.

The stars and vortexes had much to say. Eliaflore stayed with them for hours until they told her it was time to sleep. She was so earnest about learning that she would have stayed up all night. She didn't need to, though, as her dreams were full.

A shaft of light shone through the window. Eliaflore couldn't imagine what could be so bright. She floated to the window to look outside and saw dozens of shafts of light of varying hues. The angel trumpets and many of the trees all over the mountains emitted a massive pulsating light beam illuminating Clarity Mountain. Wow. Just as she was having the thought she began floating through the lights, higher and higher, to the top of Clarity Mountain and into pure light. It was all she could see.

Her eyes struggled to adjust and focus, but they were filled with light. "Where am I?" she asked in her thoughts.

"You are in the light."

She still tried to see.

"Close your eyes. It is time to remember the light."

Eliaflore closed her eyes and waited. She thought it would be dark, but her eyes were still flooded in light. She took a deep breath and relaxed.

Suddenly she felt herself shoot up, propelled by an invisible force, until she was flying through the stars. The intense speed shifted to slow motion, and she saw the constellations, the syncing, the pathways. In an instant she watched the stars communicate and knew it to be so. Then the stars and light sped past her as she was still watching universe after universe in light motion, a stunning blur. And then darkness.

"Remember."

When Eliaflore awoke, the sun was just peeking over the horizon. She rushed to go outside to greet the day.

Eliaflore flourished. She accepted her staff and position not just as a keeper of the star path but as an elder. There were many keepers, and most specialized with a particular gift: communication, education, levity, alchemy, a healing touch or a calming presence. Eliaflore was born to be more. A master healer, wisdom keeper, teacher, alchemist, light bearer, and medicine carrier.

Her understanding of plants, the natural elements, and their healing or medicinal qualities extended beyond book learning or memorization of names and substances. It was more a deep, intuitive knowing than knowledge. One grateful but curious neighbor, whose headaches had been relieved by a special tea concoction that Eliaflore had given them, asked her how she came to know so much about the plants and what they could do.

Eliaflore simply responded, "I asked them."

Her beloved grandmother Analinda left this realm soon after, knowing that Eliaflore had fully accepted her gifts and path of love. In one of their last conversations, Analinda asked her about her path of personal love. "What do you see, granddaughter?"

Eliaflore paused for a moment, wishing to honor her grandmother's question. "I see I will have a love and bring a child into this world, but I do not see the relationship as enduring. I am not sure why. Do you see it, Grandmother?"

Analinda smiled love. "It doesn't matter what I see, child. It only matters that you always trust your inner guidance. You know it well now. You will know when it is time to allow love and passion into your life. And you will know when it is time to choose to let a once bright flame turned dark extinguish."

Analinda squeezed Eliaflore's hand and looked into the eyes of the young woman she had raised as her own. Her eyes sparkled with love and magic as she spoke. "You will know. Never stop trusting what is within."

Eliaflore and Mateo continued with their work. The community had long recognized Eliaflore's path and accepted her as a trusted advisor, healer, and friend with enthusiasm and relief, like something that had been anticipated for so long and had finally come to fruition. The children at the talking fires reveled in her stories, responding to her youth and energy. Mateo and the other elders were pleased with Eliaflore's mastery and youthful touch in teaching the next generation about love, presence, and the connection between all things.

After a couple of years, Eliaflore opened her door one day to find Ikenial holding a large bouquet of flowers. They stood motionlessly as time paused for a breath or two.

"Elie..."

She checked in with herself before responding—noting her feet firmly on the ground. "Hello, Ikenial. What are you doing here?"

"You must know—I came to see you. I've missed you."

"Have you? After so many years?"

He pushed the flowers to her. "Of course, I have!"

She smiled, but not in the way he envisioned. She seemed more amused than flattered. "Elie, please forgive me. I know things didn't go well last time. But we were kids. I was a stupid kid."

"I hold no judgment or animosity for you, Ikenial."

"But do you forgive me?"

"For what? Showing me the truth? Giving me the clarity I needed to move forward? For that, I have gratitude."

"Take the flowers, Elie. I've moved back for you."

"No, Ikenial. Not for me. But I am glad to see you home."

Eliaflore was no longer a naive girl with a love-filled blind spot, but she did still hold love for her old friend. She expected him to leave when she did not fall into his embrace. For reasons he did not understand, he stayed. He took a job running errands and doing surveys for a realtor while picking up any other odd jobs he could find. A fire raged within. He would prove he was worthy of her love —prove he could change. Prove that he meant it when he said he had changed.

At first, he left flowers for her every day. When she told him she did not need or wish to have so many flowers' lives end slowly in a vase on her counter, and she didn't have that many vases, he began showing up in different ways. He showed up to the Friday festivities. He helped with the setup and cleanup. He even seemed to enjoy himself.

Ikenial went on hikes with her and showed up at the talking fires. Eliaflore was delighted by the apparent change in her friend but remained in neutral. She wasn't convinced of the complete transformation and didn't want to assume what any of it meant. Her intuition told her it was too much of a change. He was trying too hard.

At one of the Friday gatherings, Eliaflore caught sight of Ikenial playing with a young boy, perhaps three years old. The tall, lanky man sat on his knees and taught the determined toddler how to hold his drumsticks and play the too big drum. Ikenial then held the drum and tilted it at just the right height and angle for the boy to reach so he could feel the stick hitting the drum head along with the vibration in the sound it made.

At this moment, Eliaflore saw the father in Ikenial, the capacity to nurture and assist with patience and joy. She recognized him as the father in her visions of bringing a child into the world and simultaneously understood why it came with a feeling of impermanence.

The next morning, she greeted the sun with her grandfather, steeped in gratitude and questions.

"What is on your mind, granddaughter?"

Her grandfather knew her so well and likely knew what occupied her thoughts. "It is Ikenial."

"Yes, he has been working hard to win you over."

"Is that all it is?"

"What do you mean?"

"Has he just been trying to win me over, or is his change real?"

"Can the answer not be both?"

"I don't know. Yes. Both can be true. But are they?"

"You are asking if it will last, or if he will go back to his old ways."

"Yes. I have seen the father in him."

"Do you think he is the one to be the father of the child you have been shown?"

She nodded, realizing she felt hesitation in admitting it as well as hesitation to ever reveal feelings for Ikenial again after what had happened. Her grandfather gently pulled her toward him and kissed her head.

"Dear Eliaflore, we do not get to dictate the timing of love. Or the length. Your grandmother and I had concerns when you were young because your love was blind and without perspective. You had not stepped into your center, your realized self. But you are not that child anymore. You have grown into a master. You know boundaries and no longer entertain illusions."

"Then why would I enter into the relationship if I know—have seen—that it will be temporary, even brief?"

"Was he ever violent? Did you ever have cause to be afraid?

"No, I've never seen violence in him."

"Then, why would you deny yourself the experience and what it is meant to provide you? Embrace love as you embrace life. If you have these feelings for Ikenial, allow them. Trust yourself to navigate the waters. If he reverts back, you will know how to handle it as you knew before. And this time, you are better equipped."

She leaned into her grandfather and laid her head on his shoulder. "Thank you, Grandfather. Sometimes it is helpful to talk about it."

"I will always listen. Remember, just because you have been shown something doesn't mean that you have been shown everything. Parts remain unwritten, parts for us to choose. Everything comes with choices to make."

After months of proving himself, Ikenial walked her home from the talking fire. "Elie, when are you going to agree to a date with me?"

She smiled at him. "Ikenial, when are you going to ask me?"

His grin erupted as he picked her up and swung her around him, kissing her cheek when he set her back down. She laughed with him.

"You've made me so happy, Elie."

And she was happy, too.

Their courtship was fast from there. They talked. She talked, being very clear that their home would be Star Junction. It was a nonnegotiable in her life. He agreed and said he understood how important it was to her. It was his home too.

The time passed in a bubble of joy, passion, and love that filled the ethers. They joined together in a small ceremony around the fire and under the stars. When Eliaflore was six months pregnant, Ikenial found a job that took him out of town regularly—sometimes just day trips to Exton but sometimes he would be gone for up to a week. He would always return with love in his eyes and live plants instead of cut flowers. This he had learned.

But she knew something was shifting in him. When she asked about his work, he just said it was boring research, surveys, or dealing with potential clients. He claimed not to like it much but thought the money to be good. She didn't mind his absence. She continued with her life, meeting with community members who needed guidance or care as well as coordinating the Friday festivities, seasonal festivals, and the talking fires.

After one trip, Ikenial returned disheveled. He had clearly been drinking beyond his limits and certainly beyond the occasional glass of wine or cold beer they might share. His voice began to reveal his inner workings.

"I'm fine!" he shouted. "I don't need you trying to mother me."

"No, no, of course not. But perhaps you could use a hot meal." She sat him down, put a bowl of steaming quinoa soup in front of him, and kissed his head, all before he could form his next objection. Just the smell of the soup began to lure him back into his body.

"Elie, your cooking is magic. I'm sorry I came back this way. I didn't want you to see me like this."

Eliaflore exchanged glances with Mateo, who had returned from his work in town. He gave her a gentle nod of reassurance and left her and Ikenial to themselves.

"Ikenial, you do not have to hide yourself from me. I've known you your whole life."

"You are too good for me."

"I am not good. I choose good. As you have been choosing. Have you not?"

"For you, yes. You're right. I have been." Ikenial put his hand on her pregnant belly and let his head fall onto her chest where she held him.

Ikenial lasted with a renewed effort until after Edward was born. While he beamed with pride, he also slowly disengaged, feeling out of his depth. It would be too long until Edward could be taught to play drums, or play at all. Ikenial envisioned his son as a boy who idolized him, not as an infant in need of constant care.

He began leaving again for work—to meet potential partners or clients or to make deals and strike gold. He said he went to provide for them, his family, to prove himself again though she had never asked it of him. He was away and missed Edward's first words and steps, and hid the anger that arose when it happened without him.

By the time Edward was nearly a year old, Eliaflore was not only quite used to Ikenial being gone, but she had also been fielding many reports of him cheating friends and neighbors with "special opportunities" and "investments." She knew, too, that he had been with other women. During one of those absences, on a quiet spring morning, Eliaflore and Mateo sat quietly in their gratitude. Edward was content on his mother's chest as the sun brought light to the day. Mateo felt in his heart the tear that fell from his granddaughter's eye.

"Why do you hold your tears so tightly, granddaughter? It is best to let them flow."

"I had truly hoped that our window of time would be larger."

Mateo let her find her words.

"A part of me feels foolish for that."

"Foolish?" Mateo laughed with compassion. "Are there not many songs and poems about just that?"

Eliaflore smiled as her tears fell. "I know it is time to let him go. It will only get worse from here. I've watched his light diminish. At first, I thought I could help him, protect him. Oh, Grandfather, is that how you felt when I was so determined to follow him to Phoenix?"

"Learning to let others walk their paths is one of more challenging lessons, and it comes to us in many forms."

They let the quiet sink deep into their breath.

Mateo continued, "I know your heart is hurting, dear Eliaflore, with the desire for enduring romantic love, the resistance to release the attachment that you tried so hard not to form. But this is what we do as humans. Attachment to a picture of relationship, romantic love, is the ego's way. Letting go is painful. Holding on, worse. Feel the loss. Grieve, and do what you need to. Protect you and baby Edward. Love Ikenial for the gift he has given you." Mateo patted Edward's head. "And know that true love doesn't stop. It simply *is*. Love is. You need not be together to have love for another."

Eliaflore came into the kitchen from the garden carrying peas, squash, and herbs. As she washed and shelled the fresh-picked peas she heard Ike return after days away. He seemed startled that she was there, Edward on her back. She watched Ike with some amusement.

"Elie, honey, you look beautiful." He tucked in his shirt and seemed off kilter. "I-I didn't expect you to be here."

"No? You didn't expect me to be in my home?"

"No, of course in your home. I meant right when I walked in."

"Ah. Well, the vegetables don't wash themselves, nor does the food cook itself."

"Oh, yeah." He plopped down on one of the stools. "You have a point." He tried to gather his thoughts and find the script he had been rehearsing for hours, but the words were nowhere in his memory. "Look, um, I'm sorry. I know you've probably been worried. I—"

"No. I haven't been." She watched his confused expression and his fidgeting before continuing, "Ikenial, I have not been worried. There is no point in worry. You are clearly not happy and have reverted to old ways. Perhaps you never left them. Those ways are not acceptable here. Not now. Not ever. Not for my son."

"Our son!"

"Yes. For whatever reason we were meant to create this beautiful star seed together. Now it is my job to protect him, teach him, love him."

"Protect him from me?"

"Protect him from influences that will dim the light he is for this world."

"I wouldn't hurt him. You know that."

"What would you do? Teach him to cheat his neighbors? Teach him that money is more important than everything else? Than integrity? Than faith? Than kindness and compassion?"

"Money makes the world go 'round. You're just too stubborn to see it."

"There was a point in time when I thought you knew the 'world' isn't what you think it is. Have you not noticed our abundance?"

"Elie...I love you. And our boy. Life just needs to be more. It's too quiet here. I never really understood how you could stand it."

"Why did you come here and stay for so long?"

"You. You're why. But I thought you might agree with me and want to move back to the city."

"I have been very clear and consistent about that. I've also been clear about what I would not abide. Ikenial, I set you free. I will always have love for you, but it is time for you to go. I will raise our child. You do not want him in your life. You will not have time or patience for him."

"But he is my boy."

"And he will be well-loved. He will know you from your letters. You will be as alive to him and present as you choose. But you will not be here. You have chosen your lifestyle. I accept that for you."

Ike sat in silence, letting her words find their home and set him free.

"I really do love you, Eliaflore. I never knew how to be the Ikenial you saw when you looked at me. I know Edward will be well-loved and taught. Maybe he is my gift to you." He stood up and went to her, putting both hands on her shoulders and then on Edward's little head. He leaned in and kissed her on the cheek and Edward on the head. "I'll leave today."

Eliaflore placed her right hand on Ike's cheek. "It is the best for all, a decision made in love."

After Ikenial departed, leaving a trail of angry neighbors behind him, Eliaflore held a ceremony for herself and those who had been bilked by him. No one blamed her or held her responsible for Ikenial's actions beyond the surface of frustration, but she felt the need to undo the ties of connection and the ceremony that bound them. She also wanted to cleanse any lingering strands of energy he left there.

First, she made her way up Clarity Mountain, Edward securely and happily on her back. She camped for the night, sleeping in the Circle of Perspective and asking for direction for the ceremony to come. They were: untie the knot of connection, transform the vows to release the bind, have each make an offering for the fire on paper to know the return of their investments and release the cords of betrayal, and one more. She would release the name Eliaflore—and all the sweetness and naivete that she embodied—and rise as Flor, with wisdom, clarity, and experience as her guide.

FIFTEEN

F lor, Edward, and William returned home after a successful and fun football game in Exton. The boys were both tired and exhilarated. Flor noticed mail in the box. It was rare that the box was used. Richard Jimenez, postman and friend, usually handed her the mail, but then, she was usually home or nearby. Her hand paused before opening the flap and retrieving the contents. Neither boy had noticed at all. They were carrying their bags and gear. Inside were two pieces of mail.

She took a quick look. A postcard with a picture of Phoenix that made it look exotic and a letter, both with the same handwriting. The postcard was addressed to Edward.

"Edward, you have mail."

"Me? From who?"

She answered by handing him the postcard. "Your father."

It said: Eddie, you should know me. Tell me about you. Signed, your father.

Edward looked at his mom stunned. "What do I do with this?"

"I cannot answer that. You must feel within for your answer."

He couldn't decide whether he was angry, confused, or excited to hear from his father. He'd longed for contact since he was old enough to recognize the absence. But the attitude, tone... felt like a command.

Who does he think he is? He can't just do that and expect an answer. Can he?

Edward debated with himself, his emotions conflicting, for two weeks. The temptation was too strong. The longing for a relationship with his father too overwhelming. He decided to write him back and tell him about his success in football, give him something to be proud of and to be missing out on. If Ike wanted Edward to know him, he would have to know Edward. But the bait came on an invisible hook, and Edward was already snared. Thus began their correspondence.

The other item was a letter to Flor. For years after their separation, Ikenial sent her love letters. He professed his undying love and practiced his charms. She burned them. Not out of spite. She burned them to keep the energy clear. No invisible hooks to entwine them again. She burned them with love, most without reading.

This one felt different. Without opening it, she knew his message was more sinister. She waited for the boys to go to bed and then started a small fire with palo santo, sage, and juniper. The letter read: *Why have you betrayed me? All I ever did was love you. You will regret your betrayal. The boy is mine. I will take him. Just watch.*

She burned this one too with an abundance of cleansing herbs.

William didn't mean to, but he saw her burning the letter. He felt like he had seen something that was private, but he was taken by the amount of black smoke that arose from the small letter. He watched as she added sage, palo santo, and other elements to the fire until the smoke was once again white. He wanted so much to ask about it, but he didn't want her to know that he saw or to think that he was intentionally watching.

The following Sunday, Edward had left for a solo discovery walk. William found himself picking at the guitar in the courtyard, trying to find chords after cleaning the chicken coop. Flor was tending the garden, feeling his attention on her. She finally came closer to him, her eyes meeting his.

"You have a question for me." He looked away quickly, embarrassed, but then returned to her gaze.

"Why do you burn things?"

Flor set her clippers and trowel down and sat near him. "You are asking about the letter I received. Yes?"

"Yes. I didn't mean to, but I saw you burn it and was wondering why."

"What else did you see when it burned?"

"A lot of black smoke. A lot. And swirling, with white and black smoke."

"Yes. That is why I burned it."

He just started at her, not understanding her.

"There are many reasons to burn things. Sometimes, it is as an offering. Sometimes it is to cleanse. Sometimes both. You have been learning about energy and entanglements. How people can connect to you in both positive and negative, or harmful, ways. Most people don't mean to. They just don't know any better. Some know well what they are doing."

"So, you burned it because it was bad?"

"It was venom, filled with anger, spite, and confusion."

"So you were protecting yourself?"

"I burned it to protect all involved. And all those I love, including the one who sent it. And yes, myself."

They sat in silence until a raven cawed in the distance.

"Was it from Edward's father? I probably shouldn't ask. I just got a sick feeling when the postcard and letter came. I didn't know why until Edward read the postcard."

"You are wise to pay attention to your visceral reactions. The energy will always show up with a signal in your body."

KEEPERS OF THE STAR PATH · 143

William went quiet again and fiddled with the guitar in his hands. Flor started to stand when he asked, "Is Edward going to be okay? I mean, with his dad..."

"This has always been a part of Edward's path. And he will, eventually, come to a decision. But it is his lesson to learn and journey to travel."

Edward's response to Ike included a picture of him in his football uniform from the newspaper. The caption read "Team Captain." The note was filled with questions. "Why haven't you written before? Why haven't you visited? Where are you?"

His mother had walked a careful line with Edward about his father. She never called him names or said anything negative about him. Most often she said something like, "He chose a different path, one that I could not walk with him." She refrained from sharing that he had no conscience, cheated and stole from many in the town, and would disappear for days and weeks to be with other women. This wasn't information for a child to know.

But Edward wasn't a child anymore. He was nearly seventeen and was determined to find his answers.

Edward and William were growing into themselves and becoming restless. Between school, sports, their part-time jobs at Coach's gas station and the music shop, and their shared project of fixing up Sully's car, they were busy. Of course, Grace and Ray had become fixtures, a comfortable extension of the family.

The older boys took Ray under their wings, sharing their love of music, carving, hiking, and sports. And food. Grace and Flor cooked together every week. It started as a Saturday plan but quickly grew to multiple visits a week, which didn't bother William one bit. On this

Saturday, the one after the Friday night fire and a victorious football game, even if just barely, moods were high.

Flor's kitchen was the most common gathering place, not the official dining table, though it was still big enough to accommodate them all and their various projects. Today, Flor and Grace were making a hearty, whole-grain bread to go with dinner. Flor discovered quickly that Grace had a knack for dough.

"You have a feel for it."

Grace smiled. "My mom taught me when I was younger. We made cinnamon rolls together once a month." Her expression suddenly changed.

Ray chimed in from the table, "They were really good. But she doesn't make them anymore."

Grace became uneasy and shifted on her feet. "Well, it makes too much for just us. Dad is gone so often."

"I see." Flor did see—the grief, the pressure this young girl felt to carry the household with an often-absent father, and the edge of something more. "Your mother gave you something beautiful. The gift of alchemy is powerful and takes many forms. To work with dough and transform simple ingredients into something delicious is wonderful. But she gave you even more. It seems to me she taught you how to turn simple dough into joy. Your brother, and all of us, would be happy and grateful to share that joy with you."

Grace couldn't help it. She turned to Flor and buried her tear-lined face in Flor's shoulder. Flor held her there in love.

"Did I hear cinnamon rolls?" Edward chimed in.

William smacked his arm.

"What? I like cinnamon rolls. Don't you?"

Grace smiled again, regained her composure, and accepted the invitation to play. "Well, if you're lucky, and nice to me, I may share some with you."

The correspondence continued between Ike and Edward, though sometimes with long gaps that agitated Edward. He would sometimes send two or three letters to Ike thinking the last must not have gotten through. Eventually, he would receive a response. Ike assured Edward how impressed he was with him and proud. He cautioned him not to trust people too much.

"They think they can control you, but I know you are too smart for that."

"Be your own man."

"You can't truly depend on anyone but yourself, so don't get taken in."

"Let them know that you are your own boss."

"Let that coach know that without you, the team is nothing. You call the shots. He is not doing you a favor. He needs you!"

Edward fouled out of the basketball game. His frustration grew during the close match with the mistakes his teammates were making: missed shots, wild passes, stolen balls, and technical mistakes. Every time the other team scored, Edward's anger grew. His typical humor was replaced by anger and accusations, but he was the one who couldn't stay in and help the team. The feeling of defeat was inescapable despite the score remaining close.

Coach pulled Edward aside, "Son, you have lost yourself."

"They aren't playing their best! They're going to let it slip away!"

"Son." Coach placed his hand gently on Edward's shoulder. "I'm sending you to the locker room. Shower. Cool off."

"But, Coach..."

"Now, son. Go."

This enraged Edward even more.

William watched Edward leave and looked at Coach, who tapped his head and then shook it no. Then he tapped his heart and pointed at William.

William understood and tried to rally the ones still in the game, but Edward had beaten them up pretty badly. His words becoming prophecies. The other team did their share of fouling too and succeeded in interrupting any rhythm or momentum William could build. With only seconds left, William passed the ball instead of taking the shot. The other player missed what could have been the tying basket. William consoled the other player.

"Hey, don't sweat it. It's just a game."

"Tell that to Edward."

"Yeah... I will. Not sure what's got him so crazy."

At the sideline, Coach greeted them. "Good effort."

They all walked to the locker room where Edward was sitting. Before Edward could speak, Coach continued, "It was a tough game. I know you are all tired and feeling defeated, but I am proud of you. You kept playing. Kept pushing."

"What? We lost! How can you be proud?"

"Edward, what did you lose? A game? It doesn't matter. What matters is when we lose ourselves. There will be plenty of games to lose and win. There is no difference between them. They are all just games. I'm proud because when everyone felt defeated and beaten down, they didn't stop."

"But Coach—"

Coach looked at Edward with compassion and sternness that stopped the boy's protest.

"Do not carry the outcome with you. This is the lesson in the loss. There will be other games to play."

Coach walked away.

William kept looking at Edward as they walked home, trying to figure out what was going on. Edward just seethed silently, not wanting to process Coach's words and not wanting to release the anger.

"What is going on with you?"

"What's that supposed to mean?" Edward was ready to pounce.

"It means you're not acting like yourself."

"Of course, I am. How can I not act like myself?"

"Well, I've never seen you get more than two fouls in a game. And you attacking your own teammates. Never seen you so worked up. So, I'd say that's how you could not act like yourself."

"Am I really the only one that cares enough to want to win?"

"What?"

"You were all acting like it didn't matter. We're the better team. We should have won easily. Instead, everyone was making mistakes, missing passes and shots. Easy stuff."

William just stared at his friend for at least a dozen steps. Finally, he said, "That's not what I saw."

"Then you weren't looking! It was disgraceful."

"The only thing that was disgraceful was how you were acting and treating everyone. It makes me worried for you. The whole time, I was trying to figure it out and keep the peace with the team."

"I was just trying to help us win because you sure didn't seem to care about it."

"You're wrong."

"No, I'm not. You've never cared as much as I do. Now it's just worse."

"It's just a game. One game. And we all played our asses off. Except we were down one man because you got yourself kicked out of the game. So, if it is anybody's fault that we lost, it's yours. You couldn't help the team when we needed it."

William's words sliced through the air between them. Edward pushed him backward, grabbing his collar with one hand and pointing in William's face with the other.

"I'm the only reason we were even close, and you know it."

Flor heard the boys come home, but neither came to the kitchen. She waited, turning down the heat on the stove and allowing time for their energy to settle. William was the first to come to the kitchen, but he didn't offer clues. The two of them sat in silence until Edward's hunger overpowered his anger.

Flor allowed the silence to continue. Allowed the boys to find their ways to words again. She simply nodded to them, and they each picked up a plate off the counter, filled it with generous portions of food, and ate. Each avoided eye contact with the other until finally William spoke.

"Thank you. Dinner is delicious."

"Yes, *Mom*. It's really good. Thank you, Mom." Edward emphasized mom like he was marking his territory. Had he been watching his mother, he would have noticed her eyebrow raise ever so slightly.

When the boys had eaten most of what was on their plates, and seconds didn't seem on the horizon, Flor spoke.

"It seems that uninvited guests have joined us for dinner tonight."

The boys' expressions grew confused.

"Anger has a seat. Resentment. Confusion. Misunderstanding. Fear. Hmm, it is a very crowded table."

Edward looked down at his plate and picked up a huge bite on his fork to hide a bit longer. But he chewed on her words with the food.

William just moved his eyes from Flor to Edward to his plate.

This time, Edward spoke first.

"I'm sorry, Mother. It was too big. I didn't know how to...or maybe I didn't want to let it go. Sometimes, I just..." He stopped. He didn't have the words yet.

"I'm sorry, too. Sorry for what I said. I shouldn't have," William offered.

"You weren't wrong."

"Still shouldn't have said it."

Flor watched the boys as the energy began to disperse. Despite their words, they never looked at one another.

"This is for you to work through. I'll leave you to the dishes." She got up and headed out of the kitchen. "And I'll speak with each of you later."

They watched her leave and continued to sit in silence until Edward finally broke it again.

"Did she just stick us with the dishes on a game night?"

They laughed.

"I think we stuck ourselves with dishes on game night."

With that, they both stood up and brought the dishes over. Edward scraped the plates. William washed. Edward put away the leftovers and helped dry the dishes. William cleaned the counters and table.

As he was ringing out the dishcloth William asked, "Are you still mad?"

"I don't know. I don't know what's going on. But not at you, not really."

"Well, whatever it is, we're friends, right? I'm here."

"Yeah... I can't seem to get rid of you!" Edward smiled and gave William a playful push.

Flor found Edward at his desk. His school book was open, but it was one of Ike's letters that he was reading. Again. She knocked on the doorframe to let him know she was there. He folded the letter and shoved it under the book.

"Son, you do not have to hide the letters. He is your father. I'm glad he is in touch with you."

"It's okay. I already read it. I need to study for this test."

"Do you have words yet? Or understanding of what you were experiencing?"

"I don't know. I felt so much rage. At everyone. I've never felt like that before. It didn't make any sense, but I couldn't stop it. I was blaming the team for not playing well enough. Why do I care so much?"

"Why do you care about what so much?"

He paused. "About winning. About being the best."

"Do you remember all the times we talked about choices and energy?"

He nodded.

"When we are children, it is a little easier to learn. And as we get older, a little easier to forget. You are going through a time of growth... which means you will be challenged. The decisions are yours to make. All I can do is offer guidance and tools for making your decisions from clarity and not confusion."

"Dad says that is all a bunch of—"

"Yes, Ikenial didn't like to listen in that way. At some point, you will have to find your voice, your way in all things. Other people's opinions or thoughts will never fit your heart. Tomorrow morning, take a solo hike before school. And take your drum or your flute. I will leave food for you to take, and William will take your books to school. I love you without limits, Edward."

Like Edward, William was sitting at his desk. Unlike Edward, he was studying. He glanced up as Flor began to knock.

"May I come in?"

"Sure, of course."

"Are you feeling better?"

"Yeah. Mostly. It was all just weird, you know?"

"Weird?"

He looked around, making sure Edward wasn't on the other side of the wall, and lowered his voice. "He wasn't himself. I mean... I don't know how to describe it. Just not rational at all. And really intense."

"Yes, he was caught in an energy that overtook him. Sometimes, energy, a mood, can take us by surprise and take us over."

"I know you've talked about that. You've taught us about energy, choosing, and being mindful, but I didn't know it could be like that."

"The good news is we can always fix it. Heal. Transmute. Laughter is a good way to shift things."

"Yeah, that's what happened in the kitchen."

"William, tomorrow I would like you to take Edward's book bag to school. He will be on a hike."

"Sure."

"Good night, son."

Edward rose well before dawn. He wanted to have plenty of time for his hike and hadn't slept well that night. He left his book bag on the kitchen table and grabbed the smaller sack of food his mother had left for him with a note: "Walk well, son." His drum strap was slung over one shoulder and across his chest, the drum behind him. He didn't know why, but the drum felt like the right choice. Maybe he just felt to pound on something. As he left through the back court-yard, he looked around and chose the path that was most illuminated by the night sky. Within thirty minutes, he had climbed and partly run close to two miles. There he found a circle of boulders nestled next to a grove of aspen trees. He had probably been here before, but the mountains here had a way of changing.

He sat in the middle of the circle, right on the ground, and opened his bag. *Thanks, Mom,* he thought. He found fruit, fresh skillet bread with bacon, some scrambled eggs, and a piece of his favorite coffee cake.

Before he ate, Edward put one of the apples in front of him on the ground. It was his offering. A "thank you" for the space. He took a few bites of food and put it away. All he wanted to do was drum.

He pulled it in front of him, closed his eyes, and played and played and played. He played until he sobbed and let out a scream, "Aargh!" When his song changed from fierce to mellow, he opened his eyes again. The sun had begun to light the circle.

He still didn't have words and wasn't ready to identify the source, but he did feel better. The walk to school felt like a new day. The guilt about how he had yelled at his team faded away. He could face them now with humor and remorse.

CHAPTER

SIXTEEN

F lor returned home from a client's house to find Richard Jimenez waiting for her. Old friends, they had grown up at the fires, telling stories and learning the ways of the stars. It was rare that he would sacrifice efficiency to wait for a person to return home. When he rose to greet her, she noticed the envelope he held. She smiled at her old friend—not for what he held, but for his desire to check in and make sure all was well.

"Does it not fit in the box?" she asked with a playful tone.

"The envelope, perhaps. But not me. I have never fit in a box." He winked.

"Indeed. Please come in for tea."

While she put the water on and pulled out a selection of herbs, dried flowers, and fruit for her tea infuser, she gestured to her friend to sit.

"Eliaflore, what can we do?"

"What we always do: teach, support, guide. We have always known that Ikenial would return in one way or another."

"Yes, but Edward... we can all see what is happening with him over the last year or so."

"You mean since the letters first arrived. I am grateful for your concern. I, we, have given Edward all the tools and support. We have to trust that he will find his way... preferably sooner rather than later."

"I could, somehow, lose the letters?"

She smiled at his offer. "But then you would invite that energy into your life. No. Edward will see the truth."

"And if Ikenial returns in person?"

"Then we will address him directly. He will not come. Not now. He would have to face all those he cheated. No. He will convince Edward to come to him."

"And you, my friend? How are you? I don't mean Grandmother Flor. I mean..."

"You mean little Eliaflore who loved unconditionally and without boundary. She is grown now and still loves unconditionally, but she has learned boundaries well."

They both reflected for a moment as they drank their tea.

Finally she relented. "I am in awareness, paying attention and staying vigilant in my presence. The path keeper in me is strong. The mother in me, my humanness, is doing her best to trust and love through it. And I am grateful you have come and are present with me."

"Of course, I am." He handed her the letter and got ready to leave. "You will let us know if and when we can do anything."

"I will."

Abundant tiny yellow flowers and tall purple lupine declared the onset of spring, which meant baseball season and restlessness from wintering. Any spare time the boys had in their junior year was spent working on William's car or hanging out with friends. For Edward, that meant some of the other players. For William, it meant Grace and often Ray. The walks to and from school now included Grace and

Ray. Edward didn't like feeling like a third wheel, though he liked them well enough. William and Edward simply weren't spending as much time together alone, nor were they talking as much.

Coach noticed the difference in their playing. While they had never mastered that instinctive communication some teams seemed adept at, their teamwork had been there. They at least talked. But now, they were missing plays because they were out of sync. The more out of sync they got, the more frustrated Edward became, and the more disinterested William became. Baseball was taking up too much time. He could be working, studying and reading, or spending time with Grace.

Coach joined Flor to greet the sun one morning. It was far too early for the boys to be there. "Hello, old friend, thank you for coming."

Coach simply nodded his response. They sat together in silence, letting the last of the night's stars to guide them. Before the boys came out, he spoke as he stood to leave, "Moon Creek is calling."

"Agreed."

Star Junction had many gifts for its residents, those who understood how to appreciate them. Clarity Mountain, the eye of the mountain known as the Watcher, the remembering place, the Circle of Perspective, and Moon Creek, among others.

Moon Creek was a beautiful, peaceful spot for secluded daytime picnics and well-shaded walks. Though it was well-loved, it never seemed to be crowded. In fact, visitors rarely encountered anyone else there, even during the day. She welcomed families, adventuring children, and those in need of a peaceful breath and break from their day.

At night, she was a place for stillness, communion, and reverence. She called to those who carried more weight than the lightness of day, needing time to reflect with the moon and shadows while the stars lit their path within. Those called to her would arrive with the setting sun and bring an offering as well as supplies for the night and enough food to share.

They had both been there during the day many times, but neither had been at night. The nighttime visits called only when one was ready and were not discussed in public. They were private, personal experiences between the ones there, the moon herself, and the stars that lit the way.

After another frustrating practice, the boys split up. Edward headed home, and William stopped at the library to talk with Ida about the latest selection of books. By the time he arrived home, neither Edward nor Flor was anywhere to be found. He simply found a small pack of supplies and a note that read: "Meet at Moon Creek. Come now."

William had intended to change and put his books away, but he couldn't tell who wrote the note or when. He filled a canteen with water, grabbed the pack, and headed for the opening to the creek. It was already getting dark, but he trusted he had what he needed.

It must be from Flor. Right? He couldn't imagine she would send him somewhere dangerous. As he approached the rows of trees, he slowed and closed his eyes for a moment. Feeling his feet on the ground and the breeze touch his face, he opened his eyes again and continued slowly, waiting for the entrance to reveal itself. He knew it would appear as he stepped past it. When it did, he turned sharply and navigated through the narrow pathway between the brush and trees. The jagged-path was carved through a ten-foot thicket. Daytime visits offered the gift of light to guide the way. At night, it was all about touch and trust.

He could hear the creek now and caught glimmers of light shimmering and reflecting off the trickling water. The creek bed was still fairly narrow here, but at least he could walk along the edge to get to the reason they called it Moon Creek—the reflecting pool.

As he walked, he noticed the water was the only sound he heard. No crickets. No birds or bats. No cars from the street less than a block away. Just the water. William found the sounds taking over his thoughts, which had been swirling between curiosity and concern about this invitation, thoughts of quitting the team, and the books Ida had given him. Now, it was only water.

Wow, he thought. He had never seen the reflecting pool at night. He also hadn't realized it was a full moon until he saw the edge of her floating in the pool. He looked up to see the moon still rising and very much full. Realizing that he had stopped moving, he took a breath, looked around for a place to perch, and set his pack down there.

For the first time, William looked inside the pack. Right on top was a collection of herbs, bay laurel leaves, and other leaves all wrapped in a cloth.

"Thank you," he said quietly as he took some of the bay leaves and held them in both hands against his heart. He wasn't sure why, but he said a quiet prayer of gratitude and for guidance, protection, and openness and blew that prayer into the leaves three times. Then William offered the leaves to the creek, who carried them to the moon. He closed his eyes again, asked permission of the creek, and then cupped her water in his hands and brought it to his lips. Then again to wash his face.

After an hour of listening to the water and watching the moon rise until she was fully reflected, albeit still at a somewhat distorted angle. William grew restless. Where was Flor? Where was Edward? Why was he asked to meet here? What was he supposed to do?

Little did William know that Edward was also sitting by the reflecting pool, growing restless and even angry. He got up and paced, looking up and down the creek to see if William was there. Maybe he'd gone to the wrong place. The note only said "meet at Moon Creek." He looked at the water again as it rippled and the moon undulated. He hated wasting his time at the hand of others.

He started yelling, "William! Mother! I'm here. Where are you?"

After another hour, he let out a deep expression of rage: "Arghghghgh!" He threw the stick he had been holding against a boulder and it ricocheted into the water.

Now he was even angrier, but he was also hungry. "He better have packed food," he snarled believing William was behind this somehow.

Edward went to the pack and pulled out everything—a jacket, some bread, the herbs and offerings he had already used some of, and a note from Flor. "Son, you are at the reflecting pool. Reflect. I've often told you it is a magical place. No one will hear your spoken voice. It is time to learn to connect and communicate more deeply. Son, you will be fine. I love you."

Edward sank back down against his boulder, confused by what was happening. For the first time since he was small, he sobbed—tears of anger, confusion, jealousy, and fear. He sank his hands into the earth and began to calm as the dirt shifted and sifted through his fingers, tickling the hairs on his hands. Accepting his offering of shadows and holding him in love. Something splashed in the water, and Edward's eyes shot open. He searched the surface of the pool but saw nothing more than the normal ripples and the full moon.

"Okay." Edward removed his clothes. "I accept. Thank you," he said as he walked into the creek to the center of the moon. Once there, he lay back and floated, allowing all of him to be supported and submerged at once.

"You have done well, young man. But why do you hold back? Your brother is..."

Edward tensed up with the word. "I don't have a brother!" He shouted in his mind.

He felt himself pulled under the water's surface and, just as quickly, thrust upward. He fought against the water, fought against not being the only child, the special one, her little prince. He didn't mind William. He even liked him. As long as... as long as he could feel better, stronger, and more loved.

He fought his own war between love and jealousy. He struggled to stay up, to stop thrashing, and then he stopped, took a deep breath, and dove deeper into the water. He swam with the shadows until he saw a tiny shaft of light. In the light he saw his mother on the mountain, him cradled in her arms, and again, and again her cradling, supporting, embracing him in love and light.

Then he saw William and all the ways he held back, keeping to himself, leaving Edward and Flor alone together. Agreeing to play on the team because Edward wanted him to. In the next flash, he saw his father, Ikenial, as he was when Edward was being cradled in Flor's arms.

"I'm sorry, Mother and William. Please forgive me." Edward followed the light up as fast as he could and gasped for air when he emerged. His body relaxed and he floated once again, gazing upon the moon.

"Your brother is not far now. For you to come together, you must communicate without speaking. It is the only way to find him."

Edward did his best to brush the water off his body before getting dressed again, using the cloth that had wrapped the herbs as a towel. Then he gathered wood and started a small campfire. He didn't think anymore. He knew what was being asked.

Flor had told him many stories of finding people, some who had wandered off, or were outright lost, some who were just needed at home, by communicating through thoughts and vibration. They used to speak with their hearts often when he was younger. He hadn't even realized they had stopped but knew that it was he who had stopped listening there. So he sat with the fire, offered it herbs and a little of his bread, and closed his eyes.

William's concern grew. *Did I come to the wrong place?* He picked at a stick, peeling the bark away bit by bit. He looked around him anxiously for any sign of what to do, listening for any sound other than the water. The contents of the pack lay neatly next to him.

The moon's reflection caught his eye, almost flickering like light codes from an ancient world. The flashes seemed to have a pattern that he used his full attention to try to decipher until the memories played in his mind. He saw himself alone at the park or playground, trying to help his mom feel better, only to catch the ire of his father. He watched the reels play in his mind, trying hard to unfeel what he was witnessing.

A voice or clear thought commanded, "Notice. See you." And he did. He saw himself desperate to fix things he couldn't possibly fix. Desperate to keep his mom alive. To have his father's love. To fit in to this place where he was alone. To make Edward like him. To stay out of the way. To not get too close. To not let Edward get jealous. William noticed he kept himself outside of it all because when he was inside, it was too painful and scary. For the first time since the year Sully died, he let tears fall.

"How do I change it?" he asked as the flickers and flashes began to come together. "How do I stop being an outsider?"

"Come in."

With that, the pieces once again became a reflection of the full moon, and she beckoned. William took a deep breath, removed his outer clothes, and walked into the pool 'til he was waist high. From there he swam into the moon, allowing himself to submerge completely before floating on his back. The water held him as waves of memories flooded through and washed away with his tears. He didn't know how long he was there floating, releasing the past and the old stories.

The voice continued, "Now is the time to step forward. Know your truth, your path, your family."

"But my family is dead." Water washed over him like a wave.

"There are no limits to family."

"But I do not want to cause problems. I love Flor and Edward, but they are mother and son. I am an—"

Before he could finish, water washed over him again.

"Your brother is here, too. Looking for you."

"But he doesn't really want me. Not as a brother."

"You do not have the sight to see nor the wisdom to know what he wants. Besides, it has nothing to do with want. Your brotherhood simply *is*." With that William was flipped over to face down into the water. "Look again."

William corrected himself and remembered Edward coming to find him that day with Flor and the concern that he showed. Once again floating on his back, he closed his eyes.

"It is you that is not allowing the connection. Your brother is waiting for you."

William opened his eyes when he realized the water had taken him to its edge. He rolled over on his knees and stood up, wiped himself off and swallowed. "Thank you."

Before long, he too, sat with the fire and began to hear within.

"I'm sorry, William. Please forgive me. I don't know why I was jealous, but I was. I'm grateful to have a brother. Imagine how I'd be without you to keep me in line! Ha!"

William laughed with the words he heard within.

"I'm sorry too. I never really let you in or let you know how much I wanted us to be brothers. I'm grateful for this family."

They sat just a couple of feet apart, watching the fire dance with the moon's reflection. Their smiles true.

SEVENTEEN

After their night at Moon Creek, the boys had embraced their brotherhood and internal communication. Edward was still struggling to understand where his anger and mistrust were coming from, but he and William were closer than ever. One of the things they discovered in that deepened bond was connection they felt even when they were not together. Edward had made morning hikes before school a part of his routine and continued them into their senior year, working to start his days in a peaceful space. His intention was to keep his intensity down with his teammates.

As one year turned to the next, William, Grace, and Ray grew close and often shared their morning walk to school. William was not the only one to notice when Grace began to pull away. She had blossomed in the time since arriving in Star Junction, adding a joyful and sweet presence to the expanding family. Now she was reserved, almost skittish. Her words were tentative and her eyes elusive. William was desperate to find out why.

William jogged to catch up to her and Ray on the way to school.

"Grace! Hey, wait up..." She finally slowed as Ray was tugging on her arm to stop.

"Hi, William."

"What's wrong? Why weren't you waiting?"

She wouldn't look at him. "I-I can't say. But I'm not supposed to spend time with..."

William looked at her perplexed and then looked at Ray, trying to get some sort of answer. He put his hand gently on her shoulder, and she shrank away and gasped.

"Grace, talk to me. What is going on?"

Grace's eyes filled with tears, but no words came out. Ray couldn't keep it to himself.

"It's Pop... He's home more. And different. Always blaming—"

William jumped to the answer, feeling it in every ounce of his being. "Did he hit you?"

Grace turned away. Ray looked at William and nodded slightly. He didn't want to tell on his father, but he didn't want his sister to be hurt anymore.

"Is he still home?"

They were both silent. William's body tensed up. His muscles prepared for battle as his rage flowed to every nerve ending. His voice became deep and throaty. "Is he still home?" He took their silence as confirmation and headed toward her house.

"William, no! Please, you can't."

He couldn't hear her. Grace went after him. Ray ran to find Flor, Edward, or someone who could help.

"Please, William." She put her hand on his arm. "Please... you can't. He didn't used to be like this. It's not normal."

"Neither had my father. It's not an excuse. There is no excuse for hitting your children, with fists or words."

"William!"

He stopped just outside her front door and looked at her pleading eyes.

"He's hurting you. I knew something was wrong. You've gotten so quiet. It's like you're afraid all the time. Someone has to make him stop. Let's see him try to beat me up." William's tall, muscular build was surely more imposing than Grace's petite frame.

"No. You're scaring me. Please don't be like him. Please." She started sobbing into his chest.

He exhaled and wrapped his arms around her gently. The storm falling from him.

"Okay. Please don't cry anymore. It just makes me so angry that anyone is causing you pain. You can't allow it to continue, Grace. I know... I've been there. For you and for Ray, we have to get help with this."

The door flew open and Grace's father glared from the threshold. "What do you think you're doing to my daughter? Get your hands off of her."

William turned to face the angry man and guided Grace safely behind him.

"You're the one who needs to keep your hands off of her and Ray."

"Who do you think you're talking to? You're a punk. This is *my* family."

"Then you should treat them better." Flor came around the driveway just in time. The man became silent at her presence. "Forgive me. We have spoken but not met. I am Flor. We discussed Grace and Ray being welcome to spend time in our home and share meals. We are learning new recipes."

"I remember. You didn't say anything about teenage boys."

"Oh, but I did. And it is of no issue." She stopped as she reached William and Grace. "You two, please go to school now."

"But..."

"I am fine. All is well."

They each looked at both Flor and Grace's father before walking away.

"Now, Mr. Smith, may I come in?"

They sat at the small, Formica-topped kitchen table. Flor made a point to look around the room at the spotless floor and counters, the clean dishes in the rack, and the fresh-baked cookies in the cookie jar. Mr. Smith was clean shaven, dressed in a button-down collared shirt with navy slacks and a striped tie.

"Your kitchen is remarkably clean."

He looked around. "Yeah, yeah, Grace does a pretty good job."

"And is it just Grace that does the cleaning?"

"Sure, that's her job since her mom died."

"I would have thought her job is to go to school and be a teenager."

"Well, things don't always go as we think they will."

"She's a young girl, and you've made her responsible for the whole house?"

"What's your point, lady? I'm a busy man."

"Indeed. Then I will get to the point. I'm very sorry for the loss of your wife. It is never easy for children to lose a parent. You clearly care and provide well for your family though you need to travel much for work. Am I right?"

"Yes. I travel for work. And I take care of my family."

"I said you provide for your family, Mr. Smith." She looked directly in his eyes and held his gaze. "We cannot abide violence, especially with children."

"How I discipline my kids is my business."

"No, it isn't. It isn't discipline, and it isn't just your business. Let's be clear about that. I've gotten to the point quickly, per your request. Normally, we might have warmed up to things, but this is fine, too. Your children deserve a loving parent. I can see you were once that, and I encourage you to find your way back."

"Look, it's not what you think."

"I don't think it. I see it. Find your way back. I will help you to do so, if you wish. I will also do what is necessary to protect those children, whether you wish me to or not. If they are harmed again, they will come and stay with me. They are beautiful, smart, caring, and curious children. They should stay that way."

He stared at Flor, his mind scrambling his thoughts and fighting to find the right direction to go. Stay defensive, defiant. Move away. Surrender.

"Maybe I'll just move them away."

"No, that will not be the way for you or them. You will see."

He laughed a little. "You are sure of yourself. Aren't you?"

She smiled at him with deep warmth, her eyes still focused on his.

"This is blown out of proportion. I never meant to hit her. I just grabbed her shoulder to make sure she was paying attention."

"Grabbed her hard enough to leave bruises."

"No! No, I... I don't think so." He closed his eyes. "Maybe. But I didn't mean to."

"Certainly, you wouldn't mean to. What would that make you? It isn't just about the physical violence. Your children were beginning to thrive, blossoming in this beautiful town, even with your frequent absence. And then, something shifted. Grace became more withdrawn again. Ray more on guard, watchful. All within the last two months. Why?"

He didn't speak. The answer shamed him. He had been home more in the last two months. Home on a leave he didn't want to take. It was just today that he was going back to work.

"Don't you realize they weren't thriving because you were absent? They were thriving because of what you and your late wife instilled in them: joy, resilience, perseverance, and deep love."

The stoic façade crumbled, and he wept—partly angry that she had been able to make him and partly desperate to release the pain.

When Flor left, they had an agreement that they would meet again with Grace and Ray. And they would do so often. This became a weekly meeting that became a weekly dinner at Flor's.

Flor found William sitting with the trumpet tree at the hospital chapel. It had become one of his places—A place to be alone, to think and heal, and to try to find his breath again. The place he came when he longed for a hummingbird to carry his thoughts away. He told Coach he needed to skip practice.

Coach agreed and let him go. When Edward came home and told Flor that William hadn't gone to practice, she sat with her angel trumpets and asked for guidance. She hadn't been able to talk to William since intervening at Grace's that morning. Edward stayed home in case William returned, and Flor went out to retrieve him.

She found William sitting and staring at his hands clenched on his lap. He watched as they opened and clenched as if they could pump the words out of his mouth and the pain out of his memories. Without speaking she sat next to him.

"I wanted to hit him. No, I wanted to tear him apart."

"Yes. But you didn't act on it."

"Because of Grace. She stopped me."

"Ah, how?"

William fought the emotions trying to erupt.

"She, she said, 'Please don't be like him.'" He looked up at Flor for the first time. "But what if I am?"

Flor picked up his hands, looked them over thoughtfully, and held them. She let her eyes soften with his. "Which him?"

William wept.

"You never hit your father back. Never lashed out, despite his actions."

"He was my father... He didn't know what he was doing. The alcohol and losing Mom... He wasn't in control anymore."

"Pain is not an excuse to hurt another. The only way to heal pain is to release it and to stop causing more. When your father hurt you, in his confused and frightened state, you stopped him by getting away and taking it out on the wood pile—the only thing you could think to do at your young age to expel the pain."

"I don't think the wood deserved that."

"No, probably not. It certainly prefers the beautiful carvings you do now. But you coped."

"I can't always cope by destroying something. Or someone."

"This is why you must release what you have carried for so long. Grace gave you a great gift. It has led you here, to this moment, these tears."

"How will she trust that I'm not like him—either him."

"Because you are not. You chose in that moment with Grace, and you have chosen again now. The doubts entering your mind have no basis. You can dismiss them. They don't belong to you. Engaging them only feeds them."

"What if her father hits her again?"

"What if? Is it possible that you are more enraged by Grace's father than your own?"

"Yeah, I guess I am. But she's a girl and ..."

"And you feel protective of her because you love her."

He blushed. "How do you know me so well?"

"This is still a question you ask me? The first day I saw you at the Friday fire, using Sir as your cover, I recognized you. We have spent the last seven years learning each other. Have we not?"

"Yes, we have. You just have a way of knowing my thoughts...and my fears."

"Because I can feel them. Just as you can feel people's thoughts and fears, if you trust yourself and focus. You are an exceptional young man, William—kind, compassionate, and wise. And you are still learning, growing, and evolving. We do not just wake up one day with perfection. We are not meant to. We wake up with gratitude and willingness to experience each day, learn each day, grow those parts of ourselves still waiting to bloom. Can you consider the possibility of offering the same consideration to Grace's father that you offered to your own? That humans fail, often. But that they can also be redeemed."

"You mean forgive him."

"I mean allow for the possibility of healing—for Grace and Ray and their father, for you and your father. For me. Can you forgive me for not stepping in and taking you away from Sully when I suspected what was happening?"

"But you couldn't have known."

"I suspected. I thought I could protect you by visits to Sully and by guiding you, but my efforts didn't stop him from hitting you."

"But I don't blame you."

"Who do you blame? You don't blame your father for his actions. You don't blame me for not stopping him…"

He squirmed, his mind darting from himself to his mother to the guy who sold them the house, and back.

"William, what if there is no blame? What if things happened that shouldn't have happened? What if someone did something that they shouldn't have done, never would have imagined that they would do, and can't undo? What if all of those things happened because they are experiences we came to have? Your father, who loved you as best he could, played a role in your life. His limitations were a reflection of his inner world, his own life, insecurities, childhood. He was never taught to be comfortable in discomfort, to be comfortable with vulnerability or affection or tenderness or forgiveness. He simply didn't have that vocabulary. But you do. Part of the reason you do is because of what you have experienced. Because of the role he played."

She stood up, and they walked home together. Flor looped her arm through William's. "One more thing; you do not need to protect Grace. Your only job is to love her. And you will do that well."

CHAPTER

EIGHTEEN

As the end of their senior year approached, Ike's letters increased. They included a mixture of enticing invitations and high-level manipulation laced with lies about Flor. Every time Edward seemed to return to a peaceful, happy state, or at least a jovial one, another letter would arrive. Instead of recognizing the connection, Edward received the letters like an addict gets their next fix. He craved them—or at least the attention he felt they represented.

Edward had learned to steer away from talking about his mother or William. If it seemed he was trying to defend her, Ike would double down on the lies and admonish Edward for being naïve.

"Wake up, son. The sooner you do, the better off you will be. It shows that you haven't had a man to teach you the ways of the world."

The team was done, college applications long ago submitted, and final exams were approaching. Both William and Edward had applied to universities in Arizona. Local meant at least a three-hour drive. William wasn't sure about leaving. He cherished learning and continued to read at least three books a week despite his schedule juggling school, the team, two jobs, Flor's assignments and household responsibilities, and Grace, of course. He longed to learn as much as he could, and had dreamed of college. But Star Junction tugged on his heart, and Grace felt like his world.

While William felt like he had found the place he wanted to be, Edward wanted to see the world. He had never lived anywhere else. Other than short trips to places like the Grand Canyon, he had spent his life in Star Junction. Ike's letters fueled that unsettled feeling and enticed him with promises of great wonders and excitement, which played an intoxicating tune in his imagination.

The second to the last day of school, they all sat in their courtyard. Edward, William, and Ray were carving. After Ray had watched them for so long, Edward finally handed him a block and asked, "What do you see in that?"

They all relaxed, soaking in the feeling of the "last day" of school, even if Grace and Ray would be returning in the fall. Even if Edward and William chose college. There were no more tests for now. No more class schedule, homework, presentations, or pop quizzes. William heard the mailbox flap squeak up and down and decided to retrieve whatever came.

There could have been acceptance letters. Instead, he hesitated when he saw the envelope inside. He didn't want to give it to Edward. He'd had a few weeks of peace and was happy. Even though Edward couldn't see the effect the letters had, William could. But he trusted that Flor was right. Edward must make his own decision and choose his path.

William came back out to the courtyard and showed the envelope to Edward before setting the letter down on the table. Edward was in the middle of talking about the last homerun he hit. No sense interrupting him. None of them could have been prepared for what was inside the letter.

When Edward opened it as they all went inside to help with dinner, his joy disappeared, burned away by an invisible fire. The change was palpable for all of them.

"Brother, you okay? What happened?"

Edward just shook him off. He didn't have words, couldn't form them as he struggled to make sense of what he read.

Flor watched her son closely. "Son, can I help you?"

And the rage came. "Like you helped my father? Are you going to threaten to have me arrested, too?"

"That is not something that has ever happened."

"No? You didn't tell him to stay away from Star Junction and me, his son, or you'd have him arrested?"

"Of course not. Ikenial knows he is always welcome here."

"Right."

"Yes, right."

"Then why isn't he here? Why did you drive him away and keep him from me?"

"I've never done such a thing. Ikenial left because he did not want to be here anymore. When he was here, he would disappear for days and even weeks at a time. Your father knows I will always love him, but I will not condone the lifestyle he chose."

"I don't believe you. If you loved him, you wouldn't just write him off."

"Who said I wrote him off? Ikenial? Edward, your father chose then, just as he is choosing now to influence you. Do you really not see it? Not feel the change in you with each letter? The cloud of confusion that comes."

"I deserved to have a father!"

"Yes."

"You took him away."

"No, son. I did not."

Edward stormed out. He couldn't hear her, let alone listen. His ears had been filled by the energy of lies.

Edward couldn't wait any longer. The conflict had been building for too long. His father's letters told stories that didn't match his mother's. Deep within, he loved and trusted his mother, but the longing that burned in him to know his father, to be loved by his father, attached to Ike's carefully crafted stories. The words were tainted seeds sprouting doubt and mistrust. He skipped his last day as a senior and caught a ride to the bus station in Exton.

William tried to step in and stop him from going. "What are you doing?"

"I'm going to see my father. He invited me."

"He knows you're coming?"

"Back off. You can't understand this. I have to go."

"Without saying goodbye?"

"I'll be back. I just... I need to find out."

"Find out what?"

"I don't know. If he's real. If he really tried to know me. If she's been lying." He got in the car, closed the door, and told his friend to drive.

It didn't take long before the guilt set in about leaving without telling Flor. About blowing up at her, and not apologizing. He couldn't let it stop him. He would call or write and maybe come back. But maybe he could stay with his dad for a while. Maybe it would be good for him. Long bus rides after rash decisions were vehicles for self-inflicted torture. Never-ending thoughts spun with the wheels. Edward managed to doze off for part of the trip but not long enough to make the ride feel shorter.

When he finally arrived to the bus station in Phoenix, he asked for directions to the address on Ike's letters. The attendant told him he could get on another bus that would take him within a couple of blocks, but Edward was done with buses for now. So she gave him a map and pointed him in the general direction. The three-mile walk felt good.

As he got closer to the address, he began to question that it was correct. These were industrial buildings, and old ones at that. He couldn't find the number. Edward looked up and down the street before finally going into an auto repair garage for direction. The owner of the garage, a stocky man in coveralls, looked at Edward with suspicion.

"What do you want with Ike?"

"He's my father."

"Really? Huh. This should be interesting. Upstairs." He pointed to the staircase in the back.

"Thank you."

The garage owner just nodded and got back to work.

Edward knocked three times. No answer. He knocked again.

"What do you want? Go away."

He couldn't believe the nerves surging through him. Suddenly nauseated, his typically booming voice wavered. "Dad?"

"Who's there?"

"Dad, it's me. Edward."

Edward heard movement on the other side of the door but couldn't make out what it was.

"Dad?"

The door swung open. "Eddie! My boy. Is that really you? Come in, let me get a look at you." He ushered Edward in and looked down the hall toward the steps before returning inside and closing and bolting the door.

"Wow, look at my son. *My* son. You've grown up well. You're even taller than me. You do well with the ladies like your old man, I bet."

Edward didn't have words. All the things he imagined talking about, sharing with his dad, weren't finding their way to words. He may have been a little distracted by the apartment. It was both a mess and stunning with every gadget imaginable: state of the art stereo system, including an eight-track player, TVs, huge speakers, shiny statues of cheetahs, mirrors on the walls and the bar with shiny gold accents everywhere. Ike casually picked up empty beer and liquor bottles, empty take-out containers, and a pizza box.

"You caught me after I was entertaining. Just haven't had a chance to clean up. But it's okay. Make yourself comfortable. What can I get you to drink?"

"Water, please."

"Water? Uh, sure." Ike made his way to the kitchen to find a glass. "Water's not as good here as at Star Junction, but it's not too bad. You get used to it." He handed Edward the glass of water, grabbed himself a beer, and sat on the white leather arm chair. "You sure you don't want a beer?"

"No thank you. Water is good for now."

"So, Eddie my boy, what brings you?"

Edward didn't know what to say. He thought all the letters meant he was invited. "Well, all your letters. I thought we should meet. And, well, get to know each other. Isn't that what you wanted? For me to come and visit?"

Ike hadn't actually thought it through. His goal had been to steal Edward away from Flor, to poison the relationship, not to have a dependent. "Absolutely, son. I'm thrilled you're here. We have to make your visit a good one."

Within a week, Ike had Edward helping out at the garage. Edward knew he wasn't getting paid. It was more of an "apprentice" thing that Ike convinced him was a good idea. What Edward didn't know was that he was actually working off some of Ike's debt and paying his rent. When Edward wasn't working at the garage, Ike took him around town to show him off.

Edward was the main attraction at all of Ike's favorite hangouts —the bars, lounges, dance clubs, and pawn shop. Ike couldn't brag enough about his star athlete. Edward soaked in every bit of attention and praise. But he learned quickly not to respond to the flirtatious women. Ike did not want competition from his son.

After the third week, Edward sent a letter home.

Mom, William,

I'm sorry I left the way I did. I hope you can understand. Things are going well. Dad is a very popular and successful guy. I'm learning a lot. Everything is different here. I'm learning more about auto repair. Dad got me an apprenticeship. Maybe when I come home, I'll be an even better mechanic than William. Well, not sure how long. It's different here.

Love, Edward

William just looked at Flor when they finished reading the letter.

"You have something to say, William?"

"Why aren't we doing anything?"

"What can we do? Edward must learn this and make his decision by himself. If I try to interfere, it could push him farther away."

"You can't let Ikenial win."

"It is not that simple. My intention is that my son doesn't lose."

"Why didn't you just tell him about Ikenial or let the others tell him? I know there are others in this town would be more than happy to share their experiences of him."

"Yes, they would. But it would not help. Ikenial has planted seeds that will only sprout more doubts if people start talking. Edward would stop trusting everyone because that is what Ikenial is trying to manifest."

"I'm sorry. I know this can't be easy for you. I sometimes forget that you have feelings, too."

"I do." She looked down when she said it.

William had never seen her like this. "Flor, Grandmother... Mother, I'm going to go to Phoenix to find Edward."

"William, he must make his own decision."

"Yes, I understand. But if it were me, I'd like to know that I'm not alone while I'm making it. He's my brother now. I'm going to go be with him. I feel it deeply. He needs an ally even if he doesn't know it." He looked at the letter again and noticed the address and phone number. "He even told us where he is."

"You are a good brother, William. And a cherished son. I ask only that you sit with it for the night. Sit with the mountain in your listening heart. If going is still the call, go in the morning when the day is fresh."

William agreed. It was already late in the day, and he wanted to tell Grace his plan. She and Ray came for dinner, as they often did. While Flor enlisted Ray to help her cook, Grace and William nestled in the courtyard.

"When are you going?"

"In the morning, if it doesn't change."

"It won't change. He needs you."

"I don't know if he does, but I want to be there in case he does."

"What else are you going to do?"

"What do you mean?"

"Phoenix is a big city. I'm sure there are things to see."

William realized she was holding back tears. He moved closer to her and held her hands in his. "No matter what, I'm coming back. I've never known anything more than I know I am meant to be with you."

She let herself fall into his embrace, sweet, tender, and comfortable. They held each other until Ray interrupted. "Ahem. Dinner's ready. We're eating out here."

In the morning, William found food prepared and packed for his trip with a note.

"Please listen well on your journey. Your ears will hear many lies, but your heart will know truth. Travel safely and hug my son for me."

By the time William found the note and food, Flor was on the mountain, sitting with the stone of knowing by the Watcher. She sat with her eyes closed and brows furrowed.

"Why not let the tears flow, sister?"

"I know the way of things. I understand."

"Yes, but you are still human. Part of that is allowing the emotions that come with your humanness. Knowing the way of things means you also know the cleansing, transmuting power of tears."

Flor opened her eyes to look at the Watcher. The Eye had a beautiful tear forming on the corner of its lid. Flor's eyes soon matched.

"I have always known, since before Edward came to his physical form, that this time would come. I prepared. Taught him all I could. Loved him more than I knew possible. I didn't consider how painful it would be."

"Part of the gift of life is being able to experience all of it. The highs and the lows. There is no immunity from the gift itself."

With that Flor allowed expression of what she had held so tightly and set the pain free, releasing her tears to the receptive earth.

When she returned to town, she found Richard Jimenez and asked him to notify the council they would convene that night.

It was the first time William had driven his car for more than a few miles at a time, other than one trip to Exton. He and Edward had spent the last two years fixing it up, which included learning how to work on cars at all. He was torn between getting there as soon as possible and checking out the sights along the way. He compromised with himself and stopped for gas and leg stretches. He couldn't help but remember his last long road trip with his parents. The car sure felt different from the driver's seat.

Phoenix felt scorching hot to William. He much preferred the mountains of Star Junction, with all the trees and the creeks. He kept the windows open to feel the breeze, even if it wasn't a cool breeze. When the landscape became buildings, he stopped at a gas station and asked for directions. William found the building of the address Edward had sent but held back. Something told him to wait. He wanted to have a feel of things—the city, the street, the people—instead of rushing in without his bearings. He parked a little down the street and waited to see what he could. A few people going to or from work, perhaps from lunch breaks—some dressed in business attire, some in uniforms. A man with an unsavory feel dropped off two women on the corner, underdressed and on display. William thought they felt unwell, and he felt compassion for them. Despite the sheltered life in Star Junction, he wasn't naive. He remembered the prostitutes from his neighborhood in New York. Even as a young boy, he felt that some of them were caught in something they didn't want. He watched cars get taken into the garage and out.

William was about to get out of the car to find Edward when he saw a lanky man come out with a stockier man in coveralls. William recognized the lanky man right away as the man who sold his parents the shack in Star Junction. *What is he doing here?* William rolled down the window farther to hear the conversation.

"Don't worry. You know I'm good for it. It's all getting worked off. And I have a big deal closing soon."

"I'm done. You catch up this week or you're out," snarled the stocky man.

"Come on, Clutch. We go way back. Friends, like. Have some faith."

"You're a piece of work, Ike. What kind of person lets their kid work off their debt? What kind of person am I to allow it? Nah, last call, *friend*. Figure it out."

"Keep it down, Clutch. You know I bring you business. I'm good for you. The kid wants to learn. It's a good life lesson. You get help, and I catch up."

Clutch just glared at his old friend, raised his hand, and poked Ike with two fingers. "Last call."

Clutch went back inside. Ike smoothed out his hair and the spot on his chest where Clutch's fingers poked before checking his watch and heading down the street.

William couldn't believe what he'd just watched. The guy who cheated his family was Edward's father. He didn't have much time to process it because the next person he saw was Edward guiding a car out of the garage bay. Now was the time.

"Edward!"

CHAPTER
NINETEEN

"Edward!"

Edward looked up and down the street to find the speaker and then smiled.

"William!" Edward surprised himself with how overjoyed to see William he was. "I missed you, brother!" He pulled William into a bear hug as soon as they were within reach.

"You too, brother. I had to come see what you were up to."

"I see you finished the car. Nice. Lemme show you the garage."

Edward introduced William to Clutch, who agreed to let Edward leave early so he could show his friend around. Unlike Edward's father, Clutch was actually feeling guilty about working Edward so much. He felt bad that the "life lesson" would be having lowlife as an old man.

"Yeah, kid. Take the rest of the day. Good work today. You've earned some time off."

The truth was, Edward hadn't had a lot of time to explore on his own. He mostly knew his father's haunts... and most of those were bars that he was technically too young to be in. He didn't know where to take William, but they wandered anyway. He knew about a park nearby, so they headed there and picked up some tacos from Edward's favorite place.

As they finished eating, William caught his brother's gaze. "Are you finding what you came for?"

Edward didn't know how to answer. Not yet.

"Always straight for the heart of it. Ha!" Edward smiled at his brother. "I do miss our deep conversations. Always so sincere." Edward looked away, finding a couple of ravens snacking on some discarded food they took from the trash can. "How is Mom? And Star Junction?"

"Both miss you. She is holding in emotions. I could see it. I've never seen her do that before."

"You haven't come to try to convince me to go home. Have you?"

"No. I came to see how you are, to let you know I'm here, and, you know, keep you out of trouble." He winked when he said it.

"'Ha! Always the chaperone. Come on, wait until you see the place."

Edward had been talking up the allure of a "true bachelor pad" and singing his father's praises on the way back to the apartment. "He's a real popular guy. Lots of friends." He opened the door, and instead of finding friendly, Ike greeted him with disapproval.

"Where have you been? You're supposed to be working."

"Dad, Clutch said it was okay. This is William, my brother."

Ike's eyes narrowed. "No, son, he is your friend. And you know you're going to have to make up the time you missed. I won't have my son being irresponsible. You made a commitment."

Ike hadn't yet noticed the dead stare from William. He was too busy asserting power over Edward, who was knocked a bit off center.

"Yeah, it's okay. It's just a couple of hours. I'll make up the time. No problem."

"Good boy. Well, then, your friends are my friends. William, you say? Nice to meet you, son."

"Ikenial."

"No, just Ike. I left Ikenial behind long ago."

"I see."

"Eddie, get us some beer. Let's relax."

Edward found himself uneasy. He knew something was wrong but wasn't ready for it. He just wanted them all to get along. He went to the fridge, grabbed a couple of beers, and looked at William with the unspoken question.

"Water please."

"Just like you were. Eh, Eddie? Innocent, coddled. A real mama's boy."

"I don't see how. My mom died when I was ten."

"Yeah, well, coddled just the same. Don't worry, we'll have you up to speed in no time."

William was glad he hadn't rushed in. The time sitting in his car watching helped him to stay grounded now. He heard Flor's words again.

"Please listen well on your journey. Your ears will hear many lies, but your heart will know truth."

It would take all his focus to keep his composure. He was here to support his friend, not to have a confrontation. Not yet.

The next morning, William accompanied Edward to his shift at the garage.

"Look, I guess it's okay if your friend wants to hang out with you and help, but I don't need two apprentices, and I can't pay anything," Clutch clarified before letting him work. "Just, uh, don't get hurt."

Ike noticed William working with Edward as he stealthily exited through the side door. He could have gone out the back exit but wanted make sure the boys were working. Clutch was waiting for him outside. "Don't get any ideas."

"What? Now you have two apprentices, thanks to me. That's more income for you."

"No, I have one kid who's being screwed by his own pop and his friend who is onto you."

"Clutch, you shouldn't have a problem with this."

"But you should. And I'm putting an end to it. You've got two weeks to get your shit out. I told you. I'm done."

"I'll have your money. I've got a deal closing this week. That two grand is as good as paid."

"No, the two grand is just the minimum payment. No more payment plan. You pay me the whole twelve thousand or you are out in two weeks. No more games. You're lucky I'm not charging interest."

After a couple of days, William changed the conversation from Star Junction gossip to Ike and Edward. Questions like: "So, what's the plan?" And: "I wonder why Ike was so insistent that you make up hours that you work for free. What do you think that was about?"

Clutch overheard some of these conversations and his conscience got the best of him.

"Hey, William, why don't you head down to the quick mart and get us some sodas. And maybe some chips or something. My treat." He made sure to make eye contact with William as he handed him some cash.

"Sure, happy to. Thanks."

"Kid, I need to talk to you," he said to Edward.

"Okay. Did I do something wrong? I know I need to make up those hours."

"No, you don't. Look, this isn't what you think."

"What do you mean?"

"I mean, I don't offer apprenticeships. Your old man owes me... and he's having you work off the debt. And, um, I don't feel right about it. You're a good kid. You should at least know the truth."

Edward's mind raced to find excuses for his father, to justify it somehow or make it untrue. But he couldn't find the words for any of that.

"You're a good kid. And your friend is a good friend."

"Yeah, okay. I guess that means my dad just needs help. I mean, maybe he's going through a rough time."

"I've known him a long time—like twenty-five years—nothing much has changed."

"I don't know what to say. But, Clutch, thanks for telling me. I'm sorry he owes you money."

"Not your problem, kid. You need to know that. Don't let it be your problem. It stinks, but your old man—don't look up to him."

Ike saw William at the corner market.

"You should be working, not hanging out here."

"I might say the same to you, Ike."

"I don't like your disrespect. You've about worn out your welcome."

"I can't have worn out what was never extended. I'm here for Edward."

"Yeah, well, he doesn't need you here. You have two days to be gone."

William smiled at him. "Absolutely, sir." He chuckled a little. "You still haven't placed me, have you? Well, I better get these refreshments back to the garage."

When he got back, William noticed Edward's mood had changed. He was quiet and not his playful self.

"You okay?"

"Just thinking a lot." The pressure was building again, as it did before he came here.

"Boys, why don't you call it a day. I can finish up."

"But he..."

"I'm the boss. I say how many hours I have for you to work. Get outta here."

None of them had seen Ike sneak back upstairs. The boys were surprised to find him home. He was tearing through boxes and leaving papers strewn everywhere.

Both of the boys had a stunned look when they saw. "Dad, are you okay?"

Ike looked stressed.

"What the hell are you doing here? You should be working. What the hell is wrong with kids today?" he was muttering. He stopped and glared at William. "You! You're a bad influence on my boy. I warned you. Get out!"

"Dad, what are you talking about? William's good for me."

William looked at Edward and shared, "He saw me at the store today and told me I had two days to get out."

"What? Dad, why?"

"You can't just freeload here. Do you think I'm running a charity?"

"Did you figure it out? How you know me?" William knew he was goading him but felt so calm and clear about the words and the timing. He continued, "I'm a little older now."

Edward looked at William and Ikenial. "What are you talking about?"

"He's full of lies and vile, son. I tried to warn you. A bad influence."

"I was ten, in fact. You might remember my parents. You sold us prime real estate in Star Junction. A miracle opportunity, you called it. A torn-up shack more than a mile up the dirt road."

"What...are you sure?" Edward didn't want to believe what he was hearing.

"His face has been etched in my memory for eight years. I'm certain."

"Now, now, now, you can't blame me for that. You were ten, you say? I don't know what you're talking about. You're just trying to turn my boy against me. She put you up to it. She won't be satisfied until I have nothing."

"Clutch was right when he called you a piece of work. I saw that, you know. When you defended using your son to work off your debt."

"Dad, is it true?"

"Son, I told you he couldn't be trusted. Now you see how he is trying to turn you against me. She poisons everything."

"You're the one who is poison. Look at what you are doing to your own son." William wouldn't let up.

"Stop! Both of you..." Edward shouted.

William was burning, but calm. "Edward, don't let him do this to you. You are better than what he is trying to make you."

"Shut up!" Edward couldn't take anymore. He pushed William into the wall and they both froze from disbelief. William grabbed his bag and left quietly.

"That's my boy. That's what you needed to do."

Edward glared at his father, "Shut up!"

He stormed out and ran like he was training for the team. Ran like he hadn't since coming to Phoenix. And when he couldn't run anymore, he walked. He had no idea where to go. He just needed to move his body and clear his head. Where was the mountain? Where could he go instead?

He didn't know how long he wandered. Long enough to get drenched in a monsoon. And to find a little oasis in a small chapel garden with trees and a fountain. He finally collapsed at the base of a tree.

After a time, he noticed that he had been breathing the breath of life. Deeply in through the nose, out through the mouth. He paid attention to the air flowing in. And out. Then his mind went to feeling the ground beneath him, the tree at his back, and the leaves whispering. All at once he jumped up.

"Thank you!" He touched the tree and the leaves and smiled as he left the churchyard. It was the first time he had felt like himself in ages. Truly, since the first letter.

William wasn't sure what he felt in his chest when Edward pushed him, but he was sure it wasn't normal. He focused on slowing his breath and took himself to a hospital.

When Edward returned to Ike's, he gathered his things. He noticed a stack of files on the counter. Papers and files were still strewn everywhere, but these showed addresses in Star Junction. He looked at Ike, who was drinking whiskey. "How many people have you cheated?"

Ike gave his son an icy stare. He no longer controlled the illusion. No longer cared what Edward believed. "Now why would I count something like that?"

"I'm glad I got to know you. This you. In that truth, I got to see myself clearly."

"You sound like your mother. I got to you too late. She had already poisoned you."

"No, father. It is clear now that you are the one who poisons. Relationships. Trust. Your own life. Every moment you live is your creation. Nobody else has done it to you. I came here to love you, but you have poisoned that, too. I will love you anyway, but I will not be in touch. No more letters."

Just as Edward said it, the phone rang, and he answered it. "Okay, I'll be right there." He hung up. "I won't be back. Guess you'll have to pay your own debt."

Edward walked to the hospital to get William. He replayed the push over and over trying to figure out if he could have hurt his friend. Once they were outside and walking to the car, Edward spoke.

"Hey, I didn't think I pushed you that hard."

"Don't flatter yourself." William handed him the keys to the car. "You drive."

As they drove back to Star Junction, Edward asked "So, you okay?"

"Yeah, I am for now."

"Good. Clearly, I do better with you around. Thanks for coming for me."

"You're my brother...can't just leave you lost in the woods."

They decided on a couple of detours on the way back to Star Junction. They hiked and camped a night at a place called Bell Rock outside the small town of Sedona. Then they stopped at the Grand Canyon and agreed to return together to explore and camp. For now, they were ready to be home.

As they neared the familiar turns into town and caught the Watcher watching them, Edward asked again.

"Are you ever going to tell me what the doctor said?"

William shrugged and looked at the familiar Eye. "He said there may be something wrong with my heart, but I seemed healthy now and shouldn't worry about it."

"And are you?"

"Worried? No. Just aware. I don't want to waste time."

TWENTY

The aromatic herbs and flowers in the front patio welcomed them home. They both paused for deep inhalation of the comforting scents. Ray was the first to the door to greet them.

"Hey, they're back! We missed you." He hugged William and hesitated with Edward who pulled him in for a big hug.

"You weren't going to leave me out. Were you?" He patted the younger boy on the shoulders and laughed as they all continued into the kitchen where they were met with even more intoxicating smells. "Did you get taller?"

Flor stood by the counter smiling. Edward dropped his bag and went to her, taking her hands. "Mom, please forgive me. I wasn't myself. I was confused. I'm sorry that I hurt you. I see it clearly now."

"Thank you, dear boy. I am glad that you have returned to yourself."

He wrapped his strong arms around her and let his tears flow. They cried together, and he spun her around in joy.

"It smells amazing in here!" They all laughed. "I haven't eaten well since I left."

While Edward and Flor shared their moments, William and Grace did the same.

"I'm so happy you are home, William. We missed you."

He embraced her with a completely open heart. When they unfurled, she looked into his eyes. He smiled, but noticed she seemed quiet.

"Are you okay?" he asked quietly.

She nodded. In the time that he had been gone to retrieve Edward, her father had announced that he was engaged and wanted to move the family away instead of letting them finish school here. With Flor's help, he was convinced to allow them to stay with her supervision and his continued visits until Grace graduated next year.

Ray wanted to change the subject. "Look on the table."

William and Edward both looked to the table where thick envelopes awaited. Both gave Ray a hearty pat on the shoulder on their way back to the table. They looked at each other and then at Flor before starting.

"Here goes something." Edward was both eager and apprehensive. He smiled when he realized that at the top of his pile was his diploma. He beamed as he read it and held it to his chest. "I didn't realize how much it mattered to me."

"You even made honor roll—and special distinction for sports and leadership." Ray was genuinely excited for both Edward and William, both having stepped into big brother roles for him.

Edward beamed even more and gave William a playful arm smack, "Ha! You're not the only smart one."

"It must have rubbed off on you."

The other envelopes revealed college acceptance letters and scholarship offers from various colleges—some local and some as far as California. Excitement and celebration filled the air. Within it all, they made decisions as they feasted on festival stew, homemade rustic crusty bread, and a bountiful salad.

Edward was jubilant. All the enthusiasm he'd been holding back for the last couple of years wanted to come out all at once. "Mmm-mmm, this was delicious. Festival stew is one of my favorites!"

"I think everything is your favorite." They all laughed as Ray shot a quick glance at Edward to see how his joke would be taken.

"Ray does have a point." William winked at Ray when he said it, letting him know he was safe.

"That's because it is all so delicious." Edward looked at Flor, Grace, and Ray with gratitude. "Thank you for preparing and sharing this beautiful meal with us."

"I thought festival stew was only for the Fire Festival."

Flor answered William. "The festival stew is traditional before the Fire Festival and optional to prep for other festivals, special ceremonies, or teaching journeys. Of course, it is never wrong to enjoy the meal in a celebratory way. We have much to celebrate. Do we not? Do you know what your decisions are?" She suspected they already knew and wanted them to voice it on this night.

"I thought I wanted to be in Phoenix or farther..." Edward smiled as he spoke. "But not anymore. I want to teach and coach, like Coach. Flagstaff is closer, has a good program, and I would be able to come home more often to train for my master journey. For when I am ready." He was surprised at how easily the words and the decision came. He had no more confusion or doubts about future. Just knowing.

"And you, William?"

"I'm keeping Star Junction as my base. I'll attend the junior college in Exton and train in carpentry. I don't need to move away to learn. I am meant to be here. I don't know all of it, but I know that much." He looked at Flor and Grace. He hadn't shared about his visit with the doctor or what he felt in his chest.

Flor stood. "Excellent decisions, boys. Why don't we enjoy dessert outside? It is too beautiful an evening to miss. Grace has made us something special."

As they all cleared the dishes and moved outside, Flor called William aside.

She placed her hand on his chest and held it there while looking into his eyes. He could feel incredible warmth coming from her hand. When she finally removed it, he still felt a warm vibration in his chest.

"Is everything okay?" he asked her.

"That should be my question to you."

"I'm okay. The doctor said I might have something wrong with my heart, but I am okay."

"Your true heart is a beautiful one. Thank you, William. You followed your heart and showed courage and strength. You have returned with purpose and resolve."

"Yes. I don't think I have time to waste."

"Do you remember meeting me in your mother's hospital room?" He nodded. "She asked me to hold something for you, for when you were ready. I believe that time is now." She handed him something wrapped in a soft cloth. "It is yours to do with as you will. Come outside and listen. I have a story to share."

Flor and William joined the others outside as he held the still-unwrapped cloth. He wasn't sure what he was waiting for. Holding it knowing that it was something of his mother's connected him to her. They all sat around the unlit fire pit with Grace's plate of éclairs set on the side table next to Flor. Ray asked if they should light the fire.

"No, tonight is not a night for a fire. Tonight is a night for stars. Edward, will you go turn out the lights that are on?"

When he returned, they all had an éclair... or two, in Edward's case.

"What? They are delicious!"

They all settled in and noticed that Flor's gaze was upon the sky.

"Tell me, each of you, what have you learned about Star Junction since you have been here?" She directed the question toward Grace and Ray.

"I'm not sure what you mean. I'm sorry."

"No need to be sorry, dear Grace. What stories have you heard? Places have you discovered? What do you know about our town? Our origins?"

"I've seen the Eye that's in the mosaic at school. I've seen it on the mountain."

"That's excellent, Ray."

"I've been to Clarity Mountain with William and Edward but not on my own. But they said that the path can be different every time. Oh, and that the Eye is called the Watcher and is the guardian of the mountain. We've been to the Fire Festival, the Friday fires, the pinyon harvest and bakeoff, the plant and seed festival..." Ray listed them with enthusiasm.

"Yes, you have joined in many of our gatherings and celebrations."

"Sun River and Moon Creek are our way to access, work with, and enjoy water."

"Yes, very good, Grace. Have you been told yet about our origins here? How Star Junction came to be? Or what it is? Why do we call it Star Junction?"

William clasped the cloth in his hand. He and Edward had attended the talking fires and were aware of the stories, but something told him there was more to understand. "I would like to hear the story again."

They all agreed with William.

"Very well. There is much study in this world of the skies: galaxies, star systems, constellations, black holes, planets. They call it space, which is an interesting metaphor. They even made it to our moon. We call our town Star Junction because that is what it has been called for many generations before us. But what about the first generation? How did they come to be here? The legend is told that the first generation called it Star Junction because that is what it is. The junction of stars that brought them. That brought us."

Flor sipped her tea and allowed the words to settle. "There are many such junctions. The ancient ones came to settle in many places around the earth. To all the continents and to places that are now labeled countries. They weren't then. We, they, didn't have imposed boundaries. They came and went through the portals and shared experiences from one junction to the next."

"Can they still do that?" William asked.

"Yes. A few still can—under the right circumstances."

"Well, what happened? Why did it change?"

"That is a good question, Grace. It is thought that the heavier frequency here interfered with communication, or, more specifically, connection. As new generations were created, generations that had never known any other place, attachments formed—to what they thought they knew, could see and touch and speak. Languages developed separately. Lands, regions, territories were labeled and claimed. Differences became feared instead of cherished. Soon, there were only a few left that remembered the ways. The truth.

"Communities hid their wisdom keepers, the light bearers, to protect them. Many moved to remote places while some were able to hide in plain sight. For generations and generations, we have identified the children with understanding and higher frequency. They've been taught, protected, cherished and loved, and the role of wisdom keeper or light bearer passed to them to teach the next generations. This practice we continue to this day until the stars align to form the junction that opens connection once again."

Flor looked at each of them intently as she spoke. With this last line, she held William's gaze and gave just the slightest nod. When she looked away, William looked at the treasure in his hand. As she continued to speak, William slowly unwrapped the cloth to reveal the pendant that had been his mother's and his grandmother's before that.

"Ours is a junction of seven stars. The names of the stars are: illumination, communication, love, compassion, forgiveness, connection, and joy." As she finished the names, William was holding up the pendant. Flor opened her hands to the sky and looked up. Even in night, the light from the stars shone through the crystals, and they could see the junction in the pendant and the sky.

William held up the pendant to the sky and immediately knew. He turned to Grace and took her hands in his. "Grace, I know with certainty what is in my heart and believe it to be in yours. I don't want to waste time by waiting to ask, but I know you may need time to answer. This pendant was my mother Sofia's, given to her by my grandmother Maren, given to her by Flor. Please accept it and wear it to know you are always with the stars. And when you are ready, and old enough, and know that you feel the same, say that you'll marry me."

He didn't wait for an answer to any of it. He placed the necklace around her neck, pausing briefly before fastening. "May I fasten it?"

She nodded and then turned to him. "I can't answer the proposal yet. Not now. When I am eighteen next year, and when we have my father's blessing, I will answer you. I love you."

"Ha! Well done, brother!" Edward gave William his signature bear hug.

"Future sister, welcome." He embraced Grace like he never had, full of brotherly love and affection.

Flor smiled at the event.

After William left to walk Grace and Ray home, Edward and Flor started a fire. Edward excused himself as it got going. "I'll be right back."

Flor added a log and retrieved some smudging herbs and wood in preparation. Edward returned with all of Ike's letters.

"I don't fully understand how these seemed to have power over me, but I believe I need to clear that energy now, once and for all time," Edward shared with Flor.

"I think that is wise. If you are ready, I can tell you more."

Edward looked thoughtfully at his mother, all the powerful aromatics that she laid out in preparation, and his bundle of letters.

"Will that be enough for all of these?" he teased as she had not skimped in the amounts. He put some white sage in the fire at first, followed by a handful of letters. More herbs and sacred woods. More cleansing. More letters. As they watched the last of the letters burn, and the smoke turn from black to white in swirls, he spoke again. "Please, Mother. I am ready and would like to understand. I do not wish to fall in that way again."

"That was a very difficult time and a difficult decision for you because you did not understand that you were under a spell. Ikenial grew up in Star Junction and was raised in the ways of energy. Though he would often dismiss any talk of energy and light, he used his understanding to manipulate, deceive, and charm. He was very good at it from a young age. As a child, I was very enamored of my friend. I was blind to what others saw. I made excuses for his actions and decided he was teasing me and joking when he would say things that I was just certain he couldn't mean. See, even when he was showing himself, I couldn't see. I loved him without reserve. Without boundary. I believed he understood life as I did, that he felt as I did, and that he wanted from life what I did. Even as we got older, I struggled to choose what was plainly shown because of my attachment to what I wanted to be true. Nobody, not even Grandfather Mateo and Grandmother Analinda, could tell me otherwise. I simply wasn't open to their words. I chose to learn through pain, not trusting even my own inner guidance. I just wasn't ready to let him go. All I could feel was my love for him. By following him to Phoenix when I was done with school, I accepted that words don't always match action. He showed me himself at a time when I was ready to see the truth."

Edward listened intently and held his mother's hand. He wasn't sure what to say. He had never known her to be anything but strong, clear, and loving. "What showed you that?"

"He did. He spoke of forever love with me. He called me his soulmate. And he said everything I wanted to be true. He also saw other women. Many of them. I came to realize that he couldn't help himself, and that wasn't what I wanted. I accepted Mateo's and Analinda's guidance and gift of a master journey. I have spoken of this with you before. I traveled far and learned from healers and masters in many parts of the world. After a few years I returned to Star Junction and discovered that my beloved guardians had aged and were ready for me to make my decision. Part of that discussion included my feelings for Ikenial.

"They asked me what I had learned. I told them that I learned that my love for myself and for life, for Star Junction, and the ways of spirit are and will always be first for me. That I was okay loving Ikenial from a distance. Romance wasn't a part of it. My commitment was to never sacrifice my love for truth and harmony to the love I felt for Ikenial. This I had to be clear on before taking my journey of many days and accepting my position in the council and as healer. A few years later, that commitment was put to the test.

"Ikenial returned. He claimed to be a changed man. He was charming and playful, and many in the town welcomed him with open arms. He courted me, and I accepted his love with my eyes fully open and firmly in my center. He could always make me laugh, even as children. Once you were born, he grew restless. He began to disappear often. He was with other women often. And he had also begun taking advantage of his friends and the townspeople: borrowing money with no intention of repaying it, setting them up in schemes, sometimes flat out stealing from them. The last time he came back, I let him go with love... set him free with a blessing. Over the years the letters came often. At first, love letters. Eventually, they changed, alternated. One week a love letter. The next something more venomous. I suppose because I never replied. I read the letters and burned them. Since I am confiding in you, son, I will tell you that I shouldn't have read them at all. The energy they contained was far from clean. This is what happened with you. He preyed upon your longing and made you believe that he was the answer."

"Then he used me to work off some of his debt."

"Letting you go to learn this lesson was far harder than any other challenge I have faced. Now that you have returned, I can see that you truly have. It was a journey well-taken."

He wrapped his arms around her. "Thank you for letting me go, helping me to grow, and always holding the light for me."

TWENTY-ONE

The next morning both William and Edward were up just in time to greet the sun. Their beds felt so comfortable after being gone. Gratitude filled their hearts and flowed through their morning prayers. Since both felt her presence, neither noticed that Flor wasn't actually there. When they came inside, she was nowhere to be found. William started making breakfast for them. Edward checked on the hens and watered the garden. They ate quietly, neither being able to put their finger on what was happening. Both told themselves she went to help someone and would return shortly. They cleaned up as a realization overtook them.

"Is her staff here?" Edward asked.

William went to the entryway to check. The spot where she kept her staff along with her small pack was empty. Both were gone.

"No, pack either."

"Wow. Can it really be that?"

Without answering both closed their eyes and focused in.

It is time for your journey of many days. You have both shown that you are ready.

The brothers looked at each other and released a collective breath. "Let's get our packs ready," Edward started.

"I'm going to call Grace to let her know we may all be gone for a few days." William felt ready for the right of passage but wanted Grace to know they were going so she wouldn't worry at their absence.

Seven Years Ago

"Why is it called a journey of many days?" William asked for both of them.

"Because the journey is different for everyone. Some make the journey in as few as three days. Others take as many as six or seven."

"Why does it take some people longer?"

"Because we are all different. We have different paths to walk. Different things to learn. Skills to master. The journey of many days is there for us to show our mastery, and commitment. One day, you will each be given the opportunity to take the journey. It will test your clarity, strength of heart, and readiness. At the end of the journey, you will find the beginning."

Present

The boys knew only to start. They brought what they thought they would need. Canteens for water. Food including dried meat, nuts, fruit, and bread. Cookies that Grace had baked for their return with oats, nuts, cinnamon, and chocolate chips. Smudging herbs for offerings. Their bundles or mesas that served as portable altars. This journey would require them to be focused within, to listen carefully, and be willing to act without hesitation. They left the house by 9:00 a.m. and walked side by side.

Once at the base trails to Clarity Mountain they paused. There were three directions to choose from. Each one could lead them to Clarity Mountain, but only one was the one they were meant to take. The path they chose was to the right of a boulder that most called "the bear." They chose this one because as they stood at the triple fork and asked spirit for direction, a breeze arose from nothing to dance with the leaves of the low aspens, and a blue jay flew past and landed a few trees away.

"Thank you," they said in unison. Then they laughed. They would have to find a balance of sincerity and play, both realizing that the importance of the journey did not equate to seriousness. They took their time. A journey of many days was many things, but not a test of speed. So they practiced *walking well* and listening. When they felt the need to rest, they rested.

When nature gives us directions, it rarely includes landmarks or road signs. Sometimes a fox or rabbit might get our attention. They might stop right in front of us until we are sure to notice and then head in the direction we should go. In the case of the fox, it might be the opposite. Sometimes misdirection is part of the test. Birds will call. Leaves will shake. Winds might kiss your face or blow your hat off. It is all in the timing and the attention. Part of the journey of many days includes facing challenges. The boys did not know what the challenges would be, just that they would be tested. Flor had always emphasized three things in her teachings after loving unconditionally and living in gratitude: listening within, discernment, and compassionate, purposeful action.

By 2:00 p.m. they were hungry and ready for a break. They found a spot by a stream protected by a generous number of trees and a few comfy rocks to sit on. After filling their canteens with the fresh, cool stream water, they sat and munched on some of the fruit, bread and dried meat they had brought. A few currants still clung to a nearby bush.

William looked around and took it all in. "Thank you, old friend," he said to the bush and smiled at Edward.

"Oh, this is the spot where we found you that day. This will be an interesting journey. Won't it?"

William just smiled. "They always are."

Both boys sat against a tree and closed their eyes, allowing themselves to both rest and connect more deeply. William's eyes popped open. "Do you hear that?"

"What am I listening for?"

"I'm not sure how to describe it. I think it is an animal." William stood and faced east. "I think it needs help." Both boys got up and put on their packs. Edward hadn't heard anything, but he trusted William's instincts. He would be by William's side unless he was directly guided otherwise. But if an animal was injured, it might take both of them to help.

They walked just a foot or so apart, Edward a step behind as William listened carefully for the sound to lead him. They climbed a narrow path with no trail. *Why do you think you can't hear it?*

Edward paused with the question in his heart. He responded. *I'm not sure—maybe it is only for you, or maybe I'm just meant to act in trust.*

The sign will come. They seemed to speak in unison but all within.

And it did. Edward was now a few feet behind William. Listening deeply to his own guidance, he felt to give a bit of space. William rounded a corner and faced a narrow passage between rock walls. "It's narrow, but I think we can fit." However, as he passed through, a rock fell from above blocking the entrance for Edward.

"William, are you okay?"

"Yes, I'm fine. Do you think you can make it through?"

Edward looked around. He could probably climb over the boulder, but something told him no. "I don't think I'm supposed to."

They were silent for a moment, neither thinking they would be separated so early in the journey. As each settled into the realization of it, they embraced the situation.

"Journey well, brother. See you soon."

William continued on the through the narrow passage. The sound now louder and more persistent. The passage took him to another trail up. He climbed with the help of a few branches and exposed roots until he arrived on a plateau. He looked around and heard the sound again—loud and urgent.

William looked toward the cries and proceeded along the ledge of the rock-faced hillside at a fast pace until he came to a dead stop. "Wow."

It was the spot where he had slept so many years ago, the cave that had kept him safe and held him for the night. And in that space, he found two wolves—an injured female that appeared to be pregnant, and her male partner standing guard.

Edward backtracked from the entrance of the narrow slot of a passage. He wandered, talking to the trees and the boulders until something caught his eye. The hairs on the back of his neck stood up. He hesitated, not sure whether to stop moving to look behind him or to continue forward with caution. The movement had been in front of him and to the right, but he couldn't shake the feeling that something was behind him. He had never had a feeling like it in all of the hundreds of hikes he had taken.

Then he caught himself in his thoughts, breathing shallowly. "Ha!" he announced to himself to break the energy of fear that had presented itself. "Isn't this interesting?" He took in a deep breath and released it with a whoosh. He continued forward and turned up the path where he had seen the motion. "I wonder whose company I am sharing. Perhaps they will introduce themselves."

Suddenly Edward felt himself in a playful mood. He was intrigued and started to entertain himself with all the possibilities, his mind swooshing from this to that. A gust of wind blew past him, turning him up toward the slope and nearly knocking him over. He paused again, realizing the wind's message. He wasn't centered or grounded and was allowing thoughts of distraction.

"Okay." Edward moved back into walking well, listening, noticing, and continuing to feel a presence at his back.

Wolves. What are they doing here? William stood motionlessly and breathed. The female lay on her side, lifted her head toward him, and cried.

"Okay... I hear you. I want to help." He spoke softly. Some out loud. Some from his heart. He wasn't sure which would work and had no clue what to do next. "If you want my help, I need to get to you. I need to see what is wrong."

He moved a little closer, and the male shifted toward him with a slight growl. William paused. He moved slowly and took his pack off of his back as well as the canteen. He didn't want it slipping and startling the wolves. As he opened his bag and found some of the dried meat, he kept talking softly.

"I'm just trying to help. Okay, buddy? You need to let me get closer. I promise I won't hurt you." He took a couple of strips of the dried meat and tore them into smaller pieces.

The wolves' noses twitched as they caught the smell.

"Yeah, you want to try some?"

William tossed a piece toward the male and another toward the female. He was relieved that it landed close enough for her to reach it. He moved a little closer, never taking his eyes off the male, who watched him so intently that William felt they were communicating. Once William was within a couple of steps of the suffering female, he spoke again to the male.

"Okay now, you have to let me help."

The male tilted his head and sat for the first time.

William smiled. "Thank you, buddy."

William knelt down next to the female and set his pack gently down. He tossed a couple of more bites of meat to each, and without touching her, he searched her body for clues as to what was wrong.

"Hey, girl. I'm not sure what to call you. I can't see what's wrong. I need to touch you... Maybe you can show me?"

He reached his hand toward her but kept looking back at the male to make sure he wasn't reacting. The male lay down. William felt a sense of relief and let his hand touch the female. He gently ran his hand down her fur from shoulder to tail. The outer layer was long and course to feel, but the under layer felt much softer than he expected. She moved a little, not to avoid his touch but to reveal the wound on the shoulder she was lying on and the blood underneath it.

"Oh no, what happened to you?"

She whimpered, and he moved around to the other side of her to get a better look. The male stayed where he was, watching with his head down. William found the wound, which was matted with blood. So many questions swirled in his mind, but he didn't have time for them. Not yet. He washed the wound with water from his canteen, trying to see what was there. He found the torn flesh but couldn't really see more. He suddenly felt in so over his head.

Flor would know what to do—how to help. He felt panic flood his body.

"I'm sorry. I don't know what to do." He closed his eyes and focused his breath. When he felt the panic wash away, his attention moved to his hands. They were hot and felt stuck to the wolf's shoulder—like he wouldn't have been able to move them if he wanted.

Rather than tense up, he relaxed into it and allowed whatever was happening. In his mind, he saw the wolves somewhere he didn't recognize. It felt far. William was seeing through her eyes now. He felt a searing, sudden pain in his shoulder. The wolves ran from the noise they heard. Ran in the direction of the mountains and the shelter of trees. They rested a few times, the male bringing small catches to keep them fueled. By the time they found this spot, the female collapsed. Her shoulder wasn't working right. And she felt so weak and thirsty.

William cried with her, not knowing whose tears rolled down his cheeks. He felt the male nudge him with his nose and paw at his hands. Suddenly a memory flashed of Flor teaching him and Edward about medicinal herbs and wounds. He lifted his hands from the wound and found herbs in his pack. He hadn't known what to bring, so he packed everything that came to mind.

He helped the wolf—with the help of the male—to turn over so he could get to the wound better. Once she was turned over, he saw metal. *Damn.* He rinsed with a bit more water and was able to reach it.

"I'm sorry, girl. This might hurt. We have to take it out." He got the tweezers from his pocket knife, something that had been his father's, and managed to get them wide enough to grab the edge of the bullet. He was amazed at how easily it slid out. His relief was shared by the two wolves. He immediately washed the wound with more water and crushed the leaves of the two wound-healing plants as Flor had taught him. She never told him their official names. Just called them antiseptic and salve.

Once he crushed them so the oils were released, he packed them into the wound and covered it with a damp bandana. He moved around to her head and poured some water into his cupped hand for her to drink. He wasn't sure how much more water he had, but he had to share.

William wasn't sure how much time had passed, but he knew he was tired. The sky had turned dark, and he felt this was his spot for the night.

"You know, I've slept here before. I think it's as good a time as any to sleep here again if you don't mind the company." He shared the rest of the meat with them and a drink of water before nestling against the wall that had held him so well before. The male wolf lay down with his head on the female.

Edward found a good place to camp for the night with a little protection from boulders on one side and trees on the other. He was aware of, but not focused on, a slight feeling of unease and did not want to feel trapped in a spot with only one exit. It was an odd feeling. On the one hand, he knew deep within that he was always safe. But he also felt something lurking and didn't quite know what it was. A bit of dried meat, a piece of bread, and some water satisfied him before he tucked his pack under his head and looked up at the sky. The stars conspired to lull him to sleep. "Goodnight, William, Mother. Thank you," he whispered to all as his eyes closed.

William stirred. He tried to make out the form before him, but his eyes struggled to adjust.

"Son, please forgive me." Sully's voice was unmistakable.

"Dad?" William still tried to see with his eyes.

"Close your eyes, son. Feel."

William closed his eyes and saw Sully clearly, looking like he did in the pictures on William's mirror. "Dad..." he began to sob.

"I'm proud of you, William. You've grown into a good, kind man."

"I don't know what to say. There's so much to tell you."

"No, you don't have to tell me anything. I'm sorry for the man I became. You deserved better, son. Please forgive me."

"No, it wasn't your fault."

"You were always a good boy. It is time to both see it clearly and let it go. Forgive. I love you, son. I always loved you. I was just afraid you would figure out that I was never good enough for your mother, and how much smarter you were than me. It's funny the things we convince ourselves of when we are there."

"I love you, Dad. I forgive you."

Sully smiled and dissipated into light, and Sofia took his place.

"Mom!"

"Hello, sweet boy. Oh, how glad I am to talk to you. We haven't in so long."

"Sorry, Mom... I guess I wasn't sure you could hear me." He felt guilty that he had stopped talking to her after a few years. It felt hard to love someone so deeply who wasn't there. He was never sure that he got responses. Now he thought it was weird how busy he seemed to get that the words: "Hi, Mom, I love you," fell away from his daily routine. He began to cry again. "I've missed you."

"I know, William. I have been with you. We are so pleased with the young man you have become. Flor has done well by you. And Edward."

"Yes, I'm grateful for everything in my life. Though I wish you could still be here."

"I am. Son, you still hold some anger at me for dying. Please release that. Forgive me."

"How could I have anger? You couldn't help it."

"Anger from loss doesn't come from logic or fault. It comes from pain. Find it in you and let it go. You have much to learn, teach, and share in this life. In order to do that, you must clear the dark spots. Yes? All the little things that you don't want to look at. All you have to do is see them, and they will begin to lighten. You will see."

"I love you, Mom. And I forgive you with all of my heart. I'm sorry I held that anger. Please forgive me, too."

"It's already done, son. Thank you. I love you always."

William cried gently, still curled up against the rock wall. He was startled out of it when both wolves nudged at him with their noses. The female licked his face, which made him smile.

"Thank you. Are you feeling better?"

She licked him more and nuzzled him.

He looked at her shoulder. The packed herbs had fallen off when she stood up. He touched her gently, and she didn't flinch.

"Can you walk okay?"

He wasn't sure, but she seemed to say yes.

"Maybe we should go find water?" The wolves waited at the trail as he picked up the bandana, his pack, and the mostly empty canteen. He was grateful they were leading, as they found a much quicker way to the stream.

"Don't you want to know who I am?"

Edward didn't respond to the voice right away. He couldn't tell if it was in his dream or lulling him out of it.

"Or why I am here?"

"It seems that you want me to know. But then, why did you wait?"

"Because it was fun to watch you squirm."

Edward was getting a clear sense that this was not harmless.

"Ha. Why would I squirm?"

"Because you are afraid."

"Fear has no power over me."

"Then why have you engaged it so?"

"Why have you wasted your time following me?"

"Nothing is wasted. I didn't need to follow you. That is your fear talking."

"Nonsense."

"Don't you want to know why I didn't need to follow you?"

"I'm sure you want to tell me." Edward was careful with his words. He felt it was a game of discernment and clarity.

"Listen to you avoiding the subject."

"And you baiting me."

"You cannot win this game."

"Hmm."

Silence stretched for a few moments as Edward paid attention to his breath, making sure they were life breaths instead of shallow or quick. He let his attention go to where his body touched the earth and felt that connection, allowing the warmth of the earth and the boulder to fill his body. He looked up at the sky, to the stars, and beyond, feeling their light fill him.

"That's not going to work. You can't just ignore me away."

"You don't think so?"

"That would be like cutting off a part of yourself."

Edward realized what was speaking to him—that part of himself that Ike sought to encourage and release, the dark thoughts and fearful ways. He sat quietly and waited for his heart response to form.

"I do not need to ignore you or cut off a part of me. I know who you are. I know you well. It is with this knowledge that I choose to love you and thank you. I think we've had a miscommunication as we have both misunderstood your role. I embrace you and release you too."

Edward couldn't help but smile. He finally understood that the anger, resentment, and darkness he had been fighting and resisting were stronger for the resistance. His mother had always tried to teach him to feel every emotion that came, to honor it for what it was both communicating and healing. It had been easy when he was a child, but when William joined them, so did jealousy. And with jealousy, came shame.

He told himself he knew better. That he didn't want his mom to know how he felt because she would be disappointed. And despite the many heart-to-hearts, he didn't release his fears but instead buried them like a secret treasure and added to them year after year. Sitting here, now, he laid down the treasure, even laughing at some parts, not because he didn't hold himself in deep compassion but because seeing all the moments now, in the light of who he has become and all he has experienced, the monsters had become mice.

William and the wolves drank their fill of the refreshing water. William filled his canteen while talking with his new friends. "I know you are probably hungry. I'm sorry I don't have more meat. Just some fruit...that I'm guessing isn't really your bag."

They watched him intently as if taking in every word. He stopped his rambling, met their eyes, and received their message.

"I'm glad you're okay. I am too. I think you're telling me that you have to go now. Thank you for trusting me."

They both brushed up against him, nuzzling his shoulders as he sat on the side of the babbling stream. He put his hands on each of their heads and returned their affection. The wolves left William at the stream.

Edward found himself back at the stream just in time to see the unusual group hug and watch the wolves leave. They glanced at him as he approached. He moved slowly and nodded to them, offering a silent, respectful, hello. When they continued on, Edward moved closer to William and whistled to let him know he was approaching.

"You didn't have to whistle. I felt you coming." William smiled. It was truer than it had ever been. It seemed like he could feel the leaves themselves rustling on the trees.

"You are a special being, William. I've never seen a wolf here before or heard of one being here."

"She was hurt. Shot actually. Why would someone do that?"

"I hate to say it, but that somebody may have been protecting their livestock. But there are no ranches within... I don't even know how far. A hundred miles? If they came up the other side of the mountain... Maybe hunters that didn't know what they were shooting at?"

"She's okay now. At least able to walk, and the bullet is out. How was your night?"

Edward looked at his brother in amazement. "Maybe not as interesting as yours, but definitely profound."

The boys each leaned against a tree and relaxed with the

surroundings. A variety of birds were engaged in a friendly banter. A pinyon jay foraged for snacks. A nearby woodpecker was busy tap-tap-tap, tap-tap-tap-tapping. Two hummingbirds danced in the sunlight as it filtered through the leaves. A ground squirrel watched for any spilled or unattended food. Something splashed in the water. There was no call to move. Not yet. Only a call to be still. To listen softly as Flor would tell them. *To listen softly is to listen without effort. To be at such peace and stillness, you listen within your awareness and not outside of it.*

Until they fell asleep. Neither noticed the little red fox as it watched and waited. The squirrel had its interest until the boys fell asleep. It is remarkable how quiet a fox can be. The young fox sniffed around Edward's open pack. Edward stirred and the fox snatched the pack and started to run with it. It would have gotten away if the strap hadn't been looped around Edward's foot. Both boys shot awake, startling the hungry fox. They looked at the fox and each other and broke out laughing.

"Hey, little one. Sorry to startle you." Edward tried to have the same charm with the fox that William managed with the wolves. The fox backed away, the pack still in its grip. "You hungry? Why don't I share some, yeah?" Edward pulled the pack back toward him with his foot in little tug, tug motions to get the fox to let go. "You want to use your gift here?" he asked William.

"Nah, I think you're doing fine. Besides, I gave all my jerky to the wolves."

"The fox doesn't know that."

"It might." William laughed.

"Hey, little guy, if you let go of my bag, I can get some food for you. What do you say?"

The fox pulled a little more, not taking his eyes off of Edward's, and then stepped forward, let go of the pack, and sat.

"Thank you, bud." Edward pulled the dried meat out and tossed a strip over to the waiting fox. "There you go. See, I told you I'd share."

The fox just looked at him and then the meat.

"It's okay. It's not as good as what you'd catch, but at least it is something."

Edward and William stood up, realizing it was time to move on. The fox stood too, but didn't take the meat. He just turned in a circle and kept looking at Edward.

"Why do I get the feeling you don't care about the food?" Both boys were baffled by the fox.

"Maybe he was just trying to wake us up. I'm not sure how long we've been out."

"Yeah, maybe. Which way do you think we're going?" Edward felt a little off. He couldn't shake the feeling that the fox had a message, but he couldn't seem to understand what it was.

Both boys splashed their faces with the cool water of the stream, looked around in a circle, and chose to cross the stream. It was the only direction they hadn't yet been in. The fox turned in a circle again and then picked up the dried meat and ran away.

"Maybe he wanted the food after all."

The afternoon turned to evening and the boys hadn't recognized any part of the day's journey. Despite years of discovery hikes, walking well, and exploring here, it felt like new territory. Neither understood why, but both would later express awe at the mountain's vast and changing expressions of self. Both mesmerized by the newness had become silent as the day went on.

William broke the silence that had occupied the last hour.

"We should set up camp. Have a fire. Find food. Regroup and check in."

"I was thinking the same thing."

With the decision made, a place presented itself in no time. William gathered wood and prepared a suitable and temporary fire pit. He also foraged any edibles that could be a part of the meal. Sometimes, they could come across edible grasses, herbs, roots, prickly pear cactus, even morels. Today he managed some pine nuts, though they were probably from last season, and prickly pear. He thought it was unusually high on the mountain but was glad to find it. While he was waiting for Edward, he turned large twigs into skewers, prepared the fruit and one pad of the prickly pear cactus to cook, and put the pine nuts on a flat rock next to the fire so they could gently roast. When Edward returned, he was carrying a trout large enough to feed them both.

"You won't believe it. The stream is just ten minutes away."

It was the first hot meal they had made since beginning this journey. They devoured every bite and each had one of Grace's cookies. Their jovial feeling during the meal shifted to reverence. Each opened their bundles and pulled out smudging herbs and wood, once again expressing their gratitude for the meal and the journey.

Edward, now convinced that the fox had a message, mulled over the day. Although they had walked for hours, they were still close to the stream. Or a stream. He knew many were here but they must eventually lead to the river.

"I remember when I was young asking my mother if she knew the whole mountain by heart because she had spent so much time with it."

"What did she say?"

"She said, 'Now why would I want to do that? Each moment with the mountain is a moment in time, and no moment repeats. We can spend our energy trying to memorize a feature or path, or we can spend our energy being with the mountain, knowing her. The features are always changing just as our bodies do. Always remember, she is alive. You might be familiar with parts of the path, but do not ask them to be still'."

"That sounds like her."

"I think that sums up today."

"What do you mean?"

"I mean we were looking for landmarks, and when we weren't recognizing any, we started looking harder without saying that we were. I know my mind started playing with thoughts about how could I have never seen this before?"

"Yeah, mine too."

"Eliaflore has always been very wise." A voice came from nowhere, startling the two brothers.

"Who is speaking?" asked William.

"Oh, forgive me." A figure began to materialize across the fire pit. "Is that better?"

"Well, we can see you now..." Edward quipped.

"I am Zekiel. I have known Eliaflore for a long, long time," he said with a mysterious smile. Neither William nor Edward knew how to respond. "I have known you, too. Though you are not yet aware of it."

"Okay, how do you know us?" Edward asked.

"You will remember in time. For now, I can tell you that Eliaflore's stories, and the teachings at the talking fires, about the ancients and the stars, about portals and beings, are just the beginning of what you will discover in your growing mastery. At no point have you been on this journey alone. Now, I have come to see how you are doing. I didn't mean to interrupt. I'll have to work on my timing better."

The boys remained silent.

"You were observing that you were looking for features you recognized but are now realizing that those features were of a past moment."

"Yes. Though you said it better."

"What else did you notice from this day?"

"It started off well, after long nights. But then we fell asleep only to be awakened by a fox."

"Yes." Zekiel spoke without tone.

William added, "Once we decided to camp for the night, everything presented itself—this spot, the supplies we needed, and food. It all came together very quickly."

"Excellent. Eliaflore has been an excellent mother and teacher for you both. In fact, all of the mothers and fathers in your lives have been excellent teachers."

The boys were taken aback. The fathers? Really?

Edward spoke to it, "Well, I don't know about my father. But Mom has been an amazing teacher. Right, William?"

"Yes."

Zekiel stared at both of them with an expectant look, waiting.

Finally, William asked, "Why did you say it that way? About all the mothers and fathers?"

"Because everyone in our lives is a teacher in one way or another. You both have been in a circle, stuck looking for the old features and missing the beautiful changes. This is the next step for you on this journey. Has there really only been one?" He disappeared, his voice trailing off with him.

William and Edward stared into the fire as Zekiel's words found their target. They looked at each other with tears, amazed they had never realized it before. They said the names.

"Coach."

"Mr. Samuels."

"Mayor Bishop."

"Richard."

"Ida."

"Wow, how did we not see it? The fathers, or mentors, we did have. The ones who didn't have to but showed up and cared."

"William, I had always been a little jealous of you. You know, when you first moved here. Because you had your father. I didn't know how he was, but you had something that I didn't. It never occurred to me that I did. I even had Grandfather Mateo until I was five or so."

"I was jealous of you too. You still had a mother. And you had a lot of friends."

They slept under the stars, offering prayers of gratitude and asking forgiveness for not realizing their abundance of parent-teachers before. It wasn't that they hadn't had appreciation for each of the men in their roles. They just hadn't realized the depth of the roles they played. And Ida, who fostered and encouraged William's insatiable appetite for books.

. . .

William felt like he was floating, lifting to the clouds where Maren awaited. "Grandma!"

"Yes, William." She smiled with the sun and stars and embraced her beloved grandson.

"Am I dreaming?"

She smiled. "Yes, dear."

"It is so good to see you, Grandma."

"I have always been with you, often at the angel trumpets." She turned into a hummingbird and danced before him before becoming herself again. He couldn't believe his eyes, which now glistened with tears.

"Thank you."

"William, I have an important gift for you. A glimpse. You and your beautiful Grace will bring two lives into this world. The first, a beautiful girl...a picaflor like me. And a boy much like you. Fill them with the love of the stars. They have important roles to play." She started to fade. "I love you, dear boy."

Late in the afternoon of the third day, they came upon the path. It was the only one that appeared. The only one possible at all. They just looked at each other, smiled, and followed the shaft of light that led the way. They could feel the top now, feel the energy pulling them, relieving their fatigue, and lightening their steps. When they came around the last bend, their familiar top—with the Circle of Perspective marked with directions and the little grove of trees—was different. Or they just couldn't see it all. What they saw was a large circle of trees. Two large trees facing them appeared as the doorway, illuminated and pulsing. As they had done throughout their growing brotherhood, the two young men each placed a hand on the other's closest shoulder. They would go through together.

Flor stood waiting on the other side, Zekiel, the council, and others with her. She looked radiant.

"Welcome, boys. You have done well."

The End

ACKNOWLEDGMENTS

To my Hive — all the amazing authors at Scribe Hive Publishing. Together we are stronger, better, occasionally fiercer, and always funnier. Your collective light is bright and I wouldn't want to do this without you. Thank you for being a part of the Hive, and for writing like you all do.

Friends & Family — you all know who you are and I am grateful. I'm looking forward to all of our future adventures. (Where do you think I get my ideas? Well...other than work.)

Editors: To the amazing Laurie Scheer — thank you for your brilliant guidance and much appreciated encouragement. You are the perfect developmental editor for my work. And Amanda Brown — thank you for fixing things when I type too fast and can't see the errors anymore. And for understanding the fun stuff like lie v lay; laid v lay, etc.

Laura Medeiros - your covers are amazing. Thank you for your brilliant work and ability to capture my ideas and make them stunning.

And to my David — DogDad. You changed my world and made it so much more fun. Thank you for inspiring me, reminding me to "trust the story", and making me laugh when I forget and get too serious.

ABOUT THE AUTHOR

Serra Wildheart is the author of the *Legends of Star Junction* series (magical realism for grown-ups) and the soon to be released *Rebel Dog* and the *Lucy & Fizzy Adventure Dogs* series for kids. Author, reader, dog mom, nature lover, hiker, wine enthusiast, baker and cook. Traveler. Co-Founder Scribe Hive Publishing LLC. Wildheart loves hanging out with her dogs and DogDad and believes that playfulness is an essential life skill. Love. Laugh. Play. Dream.

ABOUT SCRIBE HIVE PUBLISHING

Scribe Hive Publishing LLC is dedicated to publishing great reads. Learn about our authors, available titles, and more at:

www.scribehivepublishing.com

Made in the USA
Columbia, SC
11 April 2025

56375017R00138